Almost

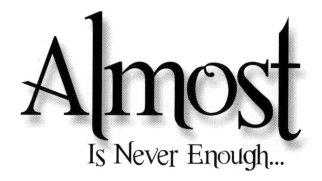

Almost

Is Never Enough...

All left to do was save her people from herself.

DHOMA GURUNG

PARTRIDGE

A Penguin Random House Company

To order additional copies of this book, contact
Toll Free 800 101 2657 (Singapore)
Toll Free 1 800 81 7340 (Malaysia)
orders.singapore@partridgepublishing.com

www.partridgepublishing.com/singapore

CONTENTS

Chapter 1   A fresh start 1

Chapter 2   Family and friends 7

Chapter 3   I see him 14

Chapter 4   Misconception 21

Chapter 5   Mixed feelings 29

Chapter 6   Nobody loves anyone 35

Chapter 7   Liking that person 43

Chapter 8   Saudades for him 52

Chapter 9   Giving up 60

Chapter 10 The falling stones of truth... 68

Chapter 11 Unaware of the bliss..78

Chapter 12 Hi I am Stella 89

Chapter 13 He never will 100

Chapter 14 Standing apart 114

Chapter 15 Rejuvenation hurts..128

Chapter 16 A little too hard for everyone 136

Chapter 17 No one knew 145

Chapter 18 A new beginning...152

Chapter 19 The final retrouvaille..163

Chapter 20 The agglomeration of belief...169

Chapter 21 The conjuring tricks..174

Chapter 22 Living with just a sparkle of hope...............................188

Chapter 23 Recollection of the past..199

Chapter 24 Without any utterance 210

Sometimes you don't know who you are in love with. You try your best to figure it out but consistently you are just in loss of words once you find out the truth. You just want to protect them and you ask for nothing in return yet you still expect them to be there for you in your worse. Stella does the same but she is still confused whether choosing his happiness will tear apart her from within or will it just make her fall in love with him more passionately? She believes in fate and eternal love but not when it comes to her, why doesn't she? Will she be able to pull through her exceptional enduring feeling? Will history repeat itself? Family? Friends? Him? Who's going to be there for her?

CHAPTER 1

A fresh start

~ Stella's Point Of View:

It's just another typical high school life everywhere. "New Year, New me" lines all over Facebook, Twitter, Instagram and what not. It seems like this just will not end. I don't even care to read all those long status's saying that they are going to change and they will forget everything, forgive everything about people who have done wrong to them and they want everyone to forget everything they have done worse to them like who's even going to consider it?

This just doesn't make sense at all to me, why make such a big deal for just a new year? I mean it's not even a new year for god sake, it's just another year!

And here I am in my room doing this three hundred word assignment that I have due next week. I'm one of those who procrastinate all the time, but this time I just want it to be done no matter what because it's been only three months since I joined this school and I don't want my teachers to see me a bad student. Yeah, I want them to see me among the good and smart students who are all nerdy, but I just don't care sometimes about it, that's what I have trouble with. I just don't care about anything, sometimes.

"Stella! Stella! Stellaaaaaaa! Are you coming or should I drag you down?!" My mom calls me for breakfast. I hate it when people scream at me.

"I'm coming, okay?! Just stop shouting!" I don't know why I get so pissed all the time. I find it very annoying when mom does this to me, screaming at the top of her lungs from the kitchen. She could just call me on my phone. She acts as if she does not own any phone when she lives in this big fancy house I am sick of.

It's one of the reasons why I don't bring my friends to my place. I just don't get it, why we don't get a small normal perfect little house for us three? Rather than being in this big mansion where I feel like I'll get lost in if I search for any of my stuff. It's so big I haven't been in few rooms yet even though it's been years since we've moved in. I clearly remember the first time I entered here. My little sister, who is exactly the opposite of me jumped higher than her actual height because she is fancy and loves jumping, won six gold medals in 'High Jump' for the past three years. Me? This house is too overwhelming for a normal sixteen year old teenager who wants to live an average life.

I just don't like it here much, I feel like I'm a stranger sometimes. The people here hide so many things. A lot of people talk about ghosts, spirits, witches and vampires here. I don't even exactly know the reason why people here disappear so much. Last year, one of my classmates was studying so hard for the exam and the next thing I hear about her is that she left the town without telling anyone. It has been just too weird that no one really cared which is why, I just detest this place intensely.

"Stella! It's been fifteen minutes already since you said you would come down!"

"I'm coming!" And her, I hate her so much.

The alarm rings for the fifth time at seven in the morning and I finally wake up with a sigh. I wonder how everyone will have new haircut, bags, shoes and makeup sets. I miss school and my friends a lot.

I check my phone and there is a message from Daisy. "Hey, you are coming to school right?"

"Yup, I am!" I text her back.

I turn off my phone, go to brush and take a morning shower.

I don't eat my breakfast because I don't have enough time, put my earphones on and start listening to songs and walk to school ignoring mom. I receive a text from Daisy.

"I can't wait to see him! I'll ask him out soon! I'll tell you details in school."

"Sure!" I reply back. She likes a guy and it's been more than six months since she first had a crush on him. I wish her luck even though I haven't seen him yet. She told me he is good looking and that he is really nice and I believe her in this because she herself is a very nice and jolly person. Good for her.

"That's him!" Daisy points out at a guy really fast just to let me see, he is putting back his books in his locker. I can see his back and he looks fine from the back view. I really don't want to see who he is but I want to see who Daisy likes. She's been really nice to me since I first came to this school and she is one of my very close friends right now. He turns around, we act like we aren't looking at him and that I'm not judging his appearance which I am.

I see him. He is fine. I think I've seen him before, but I don't know where maybe in some random class? I have seen him in the hallways. He looks nice and warm. I would never date a guy like that though. Pretty sure Daisy's taste and my taste in guys are way different. Appearance is not the only thing we search for when we like someone, right? We should know them and feel the electricity thing between us like we are linked from within, kind of.

I am a very melodramatic person, I recently broke up with my boyfriend and I feel bored when people talk to me about their crush, but I know how it feels to love somebody so much and admire him like he is the only reason you smile. I get too cheesy sometimes.

Things are going so well. I love my life at the moment. I have just returned back to my home from a house party in Barney's place. Her parents are out of town for some business work so she called out some of our group girls to her place. Her house is very cozy and beautiful. I saw him there the guy Daisy has a crush on. He looked like a very raw person who didn't smile at anyone in the party and just sat in a corner with some of his friends playing Xbox or something like that. I don't know anything about games, that's what happens if we don't have any guy sibling, we don't know anything.

His name is Dylan, I heard it from Andrea one of my friends. I find it strange that I've never seen him in any of these house party's before until now.

Daisy told me she wasn't feeling well and she couldn't make it to the party. We played all those truths and dare games and a few guys got drunk, none of the girls actually drank much except for Melanie. She started dancing and I just left after watching the scene of Melanie and Nathan making out. Andrea was sitting right next to me and she is one of the girls who go to parties and as much as I have noticed she doesn't get wasted. She's one of those students who get straight A's without any doubt. She told me Nathan likes Melanie a lot since they were in ninth grade when Melanie first started talking to him at school because of a dare. It was Nathan's first time having any conversation with anyone at school since he joined and he fell in love with her, how cute but Melanie on the other end does not give a shit. Nathan always drives her back home, even though she might have been dating with five dudes in a row, teenagers. They simply don't know what they are doing.

I wish there was someone like Nathan for me, someone who would actually be there for me. As I turned right, I could see Dylan looking at me from the group of guys he was with. Are they talking about me? Why would he look at me? Might be because I am a friend of Daisy's? Yeah, that must be the only reason. He is kind of charming when he smiles even though he barely does. I've never seen him laugh. For a minute, I wanted to ask Daisy if she has ever seen him laugh and I do. I slowly grab my phone and text her. I don't know why I am so curious about this anonymous guy my friend likes.

"Have you ever seen your crush laughing?"

"Yes, I did."

Oh. He does laugh then.

It was about midnight and I had to leave the house. I told my mom that I would be back before twelve. As I was walking on my way to my house after bidding bye to every one of my friends, I started thinking about my ex-boyfriend, Evan.

I recently broke up with him. He is a really sweet guy who he likes me a lot, but because we are in different cities it makes no sense talking on Skype every day. He told me he would come visit me soon but now we aren't together so I think he won't. I don't know what to tell him, but I just want to call him. The moment when I dial his number I see someone on the right side of the road in a gray hoodie and blue jeans with a sneaker. I think he is someone from the party, but I don't really bother. On the third ring, Evan answers.

"Hey..?" His voice sounds sleepy. It's two in the morning anyways he must have been sleeping. I shouldn't have called. I'm really stupid.

"Hey, If you were sleeping, then you can go back to sleep. I don't want to bother you." I tell him. Shit. Why did I even say that? I am such a fool; I wanted to talk to him.

"It's ok Stella. I'm awake now. Is anything wrong?" He is really sweet.

"Yeah, I just missed you. I'm on my way to my home though. I went to a house party at one of my friend's place. I'm really tired." I answer with a sigh. Well, I am. I just feel all worked up for breaking up with him.

"Oh. So how was it?" He asked.

"It was fine. Until the same Melanie girl started dancing like nuts." We both laughed hard. I've told him about her a lot of times already. She is a major diva, not.

"You shouldn't be out late much. Anything can happen, you know? You should be careful."

He is louder. I hate it when he becomes over protective. I'm a girl so I shouldn't be out late? I feel annoyed by the sound of that "Anything can happen, you know? You should be careful."

"It's okay. This place is different than the place where you live at. There are plenty of people walking around." I lie. There's only me, but I just have to make him shut. Even if I sound rude, I just am that way. I am a feminist, in a way because in the past, I have forced my parents to vote only to women standing up for politics because it is rare. I mean, it is somehow feminist, I hope.

He clears his throat and slowly he asks, "Okay then. So you want to give us another try?" Why does he always think that way?

"No! Evan... You know me well. We are over it already and I think it's best for both of us." My voice sounding annoyed.

"Yeah, I know. We had a really unhealthy relationship. Or are you seeing another guy?"

"No! I just broke up with you a few months back." I answer him as fast as I can.

"But by the way you sound. I feel like you have a crush or something on someone." He is probably sad because I said no right away when he asked. I always make a fool out of myself.

"Do I?" I ask him. I don't know. I don't, right? Yeah, I don't.

"Yes, you do."

He almost whispers.

CHAPTER 2

Family and friends

"I don't." I hang up on him.

I just called him after an entire work piled up week. And he tells me that I'm in love with someone? What does he think of himself? He thinks he knows me well? We dated only for a year! He doesn't know shit about me.

I hear a fake cough from behind as I turn around to see the person, it's him.

Crap! The last person I wanted to see, Dylan. Was I too loud? I don't think so, though.

I see him staring at me, but I try to ignore the awkward eye contact we were having. I turn around ignoring his presence and walk fast to my home.

What's his problem? Why did he fake cough on me? Was he stalking me? No, why would he? Was he trying to flirt? What the hell? No! He would never do that. Damn his eyes are so suspicious. I don't want to think about him anyways, I should keep my thoughts of him away from me. Daisy told me he was nice so maybe he is.

I can't complain, I just don't know him well that's it.

"I don't want to drive her to school!" I tell my mom nearly shouting.

"Stella, I have to go right away to my office. I have no other option than to hand her to you. You guys attend the same school anyways." She smiles at me. I don't answer. I don't want to. She knows I don't want to drop her. I don't know where my mom goes almost once in every month.

"She's your sister." Mom softly adds.

"She's my STEP-sister." I remind her emphasizing STEP. She raises her eyebrows.

I hate her so much. Why had she even broken up with dad? Even though, I don't mind Grace. She is just thirteen years old and she has so many other things to worry about during this fragile teenager stage, I don't want to hurt her but I just don't want to be with her. She is smart, cute, bubbly, and talented but she is not my dad's daughter and that would mean that she is not my sister as well.

I've always loved my dad more than anything else in my life. I mean well, I liked a guy more when I was in ninth grade, my first boyfriend. No one can forget their first boyfriend they say maybe that's true, but I don't know about me. I don't even remember the times I have spent with him. Maybe he wasn't the right guy for me.

Wait, what the hell was I thinking about? I have to be mad at mom right now and not think about my first boyfriend.

I pull Grace's arm and push her in the car just to show mom how less I care about her daughter. I tell my half-sister loud and clearly, "Just stay here and don't move." So that mom could hear it too.

As soon as I start the car and look at mom, she's not there anymore. That was quick.

Grace quietly nods and looks at her phone. Thank you so much for being such a nice sister I sarcastically tell myself.

After an awkward long silence that we were having I break to my sister "Are you really dating that kid? What was his name again?"

"Blake." She says without getting mad at me for I forgot his name. I look through the mirror and I could see that she is still busy with her phone texting someone maybe or tweeting some shit. I sigh.

"Right, Blake. He is in one of my classes, History?"

"I know" her answers are shorter than it used to be. He has really influenced her. I don't really like that dude, to be honest. All the girls know him and as weird as it sounds, I just don't like the idea of my sister dating a guy of my age. It just sounds so wrong to me.

I mean, she can even fall in love with my boyfriend in the future? What am I even thinking about? I know my sister likes older boys, but she would never date any guy I like. Well, she did once, but that was a long time back and she just wanted to date someone at that time. I can forget that thing now because he was a few months younger than me? Around eight months younger? So, it's quite obvious that my sister can like him too as his age is closer to her as well.

"Get off the car." I tell her as soon as we reach the parking lot.

She rolls her eyes and leaves the car pushing the door hard.

Did she come to know that I've been thinking about all these stupid stuff? Hope she didn't.

"He- what?!" I scream at Daisy.

"He's been ignoring me for a few days now. It's almost been a week. He doesn't reply to any of my messages. I don't like him anymore. He thinks I want him really bad, but now I don't. "She's almost crying, but she bites her tongue and tries to stop her tear from falling.

"He looks like a really mean guy so you actually don't need to feel bad about him." I tell her the truth. How I feel about him. I feel like he is mean and rude and screwed up.

"Yeah, he is really mean." She slowly agrees.

"Ok Daisy, to make it all clear to you actually he is just not worth you. You've liked him for so long and you even asked him out. You guys went out together, but now he doesn't reply your messages? He just proved that he is a douchebag."

She is quite. So am I. I don't know him, why do I hate him so much? I have so much hatred towards him. Maybe it's because he made my friend feel bad. He broke her heart actually. I consider ignoring messages as one of the worse things a girl can handle or get through. I mean well not be proud of but I don't remember any guy who has ever ignored mine, but if they do, I would feel like a loser and that I'm not worth their time for replying.

It's been a week since the school started and I'm already in my bad days as I have to see Daisy every day from now on and I just can't see her sad, unhappy about something that wasn't worth her time. He wasn't worth her.

"I'm sorry about everything, Daisy." I really am. I'm really mad at that guy though. I feel like telling him how much it hurts when you feel all ignored by the person you are dying to get along with. I want to teach him a lesson for this. I want him to know how much everything hurts. It seems like he hasn't seen the bad things in life, about love, he has yet to see.

"No, it's okay. He is mean and will always be mean. I can't change that." She is on my side of hating him. She will get through it. I know that she is strong.

Emma, Chloe and Sydney walk by and Daisy smiles at them hiding everything that's going wrong with her.

Sydney says aloud, "Jonathan's place tonight! Don't forget to tag along, girls. I'll text you guys his address right away."

Another house party.

"Is there any reason?" I ask.

"Yeah, someone from our school is leaving next week so Jonathon's throwing a party for that dude. It won't really be exciting, but yeah, better than sleeping in the night of the first week of school." Chloe answers with a smirk.

Chloe stands next to me and asks me how things are going with me. I smile slowly and give her a sign saying that I'll tell her later. She is my best friend and she is one of the best girls if you get to know her.

Well, even Emma is one of my best-friend, but I'm closer to Chloe. Sydney is one of my close friends and she is always in a happy mood. You can see her smiling all the time, but you know everyone has their own story. Everyone has someone or something in their life to worry about and I believe all of my friends do as well. They just don't show, like me.

After talking with the group for almost an hour me and Chloe, we go to her house to get her change her dress for tonight. I tell her about my boyfriend's - my EX boyfriend's question he asked me last week. Since then I haven't called him, but he keeps on texting me. I haven't read any of his texts, except for a few, but I didn't reply. He said he was sorry and that he might have misunderstood for the way I talked that night. Well calling him all of a sudden is somehow weird and stupid of me to even do that as he is my ex-boyfriend not the current one.

He knows me very well, though. I really love him for that. He always used to tell me that I'm very pretty and perfect which isn't true, but he being sweet and a good boyfriend at that time meant a lot to me but things are different now. I don't want him to be sweet towards me and I don't want him to think that he is the only guy who knows me well.

Chloe tells me to ignore him as much as I can for this coming week as well. She told me I shouldn't be contacting him every now and then and yeah, it's true, I shouldn't.

I pick out a black dress from the closet for Chloe that we bought last week and her curves look amazing in it. I would curse her for having such an amazing figure and damn those legs are perfect. She is slim and her height is perfect too. I wonder what I'll be wearing tonight, I don't really want to go to any party, though but I should forget what happened and move on with my life. I was the one who broke up with Evan. I shouldn't be feeling bad about it. Bad about how much he knew me.

We go to my house then. I don't know what to wear. I plan on asking Chloe to pick one for me too and she does without letting me tell her. She knows me well.

She picks out a red dress.

"Ew! No I look like a slut in this!" I complain. I got it as a gift during New Years from one of my aunts. Even though it's branded I just don't like the color red. It reminds me of a lot of stuffs... Blood and scary stuff I don't know.

"Hmm..." She slowly picks out a blue one. That's what I prefer more.

I smile and snatch it away from her hand and change into my dress. When I turn around to see myself in the mirror, Chloe is already doing her make up. Well heavy makeup. She is too much of a makeup person though. I softly brush my hair and leave it falling on my back. I put some hair sprays and perfume until Chloe is perfectly hidden under her makeup.

"Can I do your make up?" She smiles at me. I don't want her to.

"Um.. It's fine, Chloe. "I smile back at her.

"I promise I won't do too much. Just a little... Just a little? Please?" She gives an innocent smile and adds, "Pleaaaaaassssseeeeeeeeeeeee"

I nod and she jumps like a small baby. I close my eyes and I feel her putting foundation and powder on my face when I hear her singing, "I get to do Stella's make uppppp... Maaaakkkeee uppppp... Maaaaaaa"

I open my eyes, "If you don't shut-"

"Okay, I get it." she sighs and rolls her eyes.

After about exactly ten minutes she screams," OMG! You look so pretty!"

She pushes my chair near to the mirror to let me see myself.

"Shit." I whisper, I look like someone else. I mean, yeah, every time I do a little make-up, I look totally different but this was too different.

"Do I look that ugly?" I add.

"What?! You don't like it?" Chloe screams.

"No. I just-"

"I know you look different" Chloe breaks in, smile's softly at me and adds, "but for good." Do I look really ugly in reality that I have to hide myself with make up to look pretty?

CHAPTER 3

I see him

I have my car by myself today and I'm really looking forward to this party, I don't know why. Maybe because Daisy will be there? I really want to see her though. As soon as we reach at Jonathan's place, Chloe jumps out of the red car and whispers in my ears, "I've had this tiny crush on him since the last party." She smirks as soon as we see Jonathan coming on our way from far.

Wow Chloe pretty much likes a lot of guys. She recently around a month back told me that she had a crush on one of the senior.

I get off the car, pull my clutch and put the car key in.

As I turn back I see them standing together and I quickly take a picture of them without letting them know. I've always been this way, taking pictures of people sneakily. More like a paparazzi.

Jonathan welcomes her with a hug and I'm not surprised when I see Chloe's lips on his cheek. He probably didn't take it as a hint, but Chloe won't leave any chance.

As I slowly start walking holding my phone and clutch, he walks toward me and I thank him softly with a warm smile, "Thank you for inviting." As if, I have never been to any house parties before.

He smiles like a gentleman as he gives a hug and I hug him back. He is a nice guy as far as I know.

We walk in his house and I feel very comfortable. I've been at his place more than five times.

I see him again. Dylan. Shit no. Please don't fake cough on me again. He is such a creep. I keep my thoughts away and walk with Chloe.

Chloe introduces me to some girls who are sitting in a group laughing at someone. I hate them. I don't know why but the first impression itself isn't really good. They don't bother to mention their name and I don't care too. I fake smile and sit next to Chloe.

As soon as I sit there, I see Dylan sitting next to Chloe on her other side. It's going to be a bad night. The girl's keeps on talking about the people they have dated so far and how they didn't cheat on them.

Me, Chloe, Dylan and two other guys sitting next to Dylan are all having our drinks quietly listening to those girls and smiling at them.

I don't know why Daisy isn't here yet. Did something happen again? Is she not coming? I can't stop thinking about her; it's been one hour already sitting awkwardly next to this guy she almost dated. When I take my third glass I see Dylan looking at me.

His body is slightly bent and I could clearly see his eyes staring at me. I act like I didn't see it, but I just can't help it so I turn around to the other side facing the wall. Awkward move.

He probably might have noticed me feeling uncomfortable by his stare. Chloe doesn't seem to notice anything at all. She's busy listening and laughing at those girl's stories. Fake stories shall I say?

After a while of my weird posture I move and sit straight again slightly, looking at that guy again, Dylan. Only if he is occupied by something else so that I won't feel awkward.

I see his eyes. Damn those eyes. I keep on mentioning them. But they're so, suspicious. I slowly look at his face for the way his structures are done, it's perfect...

But what is this? He keeps on smiling at those fake girls. Does he like any of the girl's there? Well, Maybe. I don't even know him. He is just someone my friend likes- liked. I don't give a shit about who he is anyways.

After few hours of waiting for Daisy I finally see Daisy with Nathan? I hug Daisy very tightly because I was missing her so much for the last couple of awkward hours. Daisy says hi to everyone but ignores Dylan. Well, that's what should be done to him. Ignored. He seems to not care at all about Daisy like I heard about him.

Nathan on the other hand is a very polite guy. Don't have any class with him, but I've known him since I was new in school. Such a nice guy.

Nathan and Daisy joins the group and starts talking about teachers. The new English teacher, it seems like no one really likes him. Daisy leaves for washroom and I follow her. I wanted to have some girl talk with her and the group we were sitting with was too awkward.

I wash my hand, put some lipstick and do some touch ups till Daisy comes out of the toilet.

She brightly smiles washing her hand, "Hey." Is all she says?

I keep my makeup kit in my clutch and turn over to her, "You ignored him." Yeah, well that's what I meant about girl talk earlier.

She squeezes the liquid hand soap, "I know!"

She washes the soap off her hand and adds, "It's so awkward, you know. Sitting near a guy who dumped you just yesterday?"

I know how it must have felt. Even though I have never experienced any rejection throughout my life, I still know how it feels and how much it hurts. I hate him for that though.

I wish I could tell her how much I hate him for what he has done to her. I hate Heartbreakers, always did.

"Annoying" I whisper as soon as I see him sitting at the same spot when we return from the washroom.

Chloe shouts, then, "Let's play a game?!!"

"No" Me and Dylan answer simultaneously.

Chloe and the other 2 talkative girls scream, "Jinx!" But neither Dylan nor I care about saying it.

"Aww.. Come on! "Dylan speaks up, looking at me.

I gradually turn right to look at his face only to find him facing towards me. Was he just talking to me?

"What?" I look puzzled.

What did he just say though? Come on? What? Am I a kindergarten kid or something to come on at? Who does he think he is talking to?

"Never-mind"

NEVER MIND?!! What the hell? He should answer me when I ask him a question!

"Hey, calm down. You look pinkish red." Chloe softly whispers in my ears.

What? I.. What? My worst night ever! I'm never going to forget this night. I never blush in front of people that easily. Especially when it includes a lot of people, never!

He can't ever-never mind me! I'll make him realize that. I'm so going to make him pay for this embarrassment.

After half an hour, Chloe comes to sit next to me after all their beer drinking game.

"Are you still-"

"No, I'm not pissed about what happened thirty three minutes back when he never minded me like I'm a kid." I answer quickly before hearing out what she wanted to ask because I knew what her question would be.

"Well then seems like you still are." She raises her eyebrows.

"He is really annoying, okay?" I spit it out. I had to say it. I've controlled myself for the past half an hour and I feel like bursting out on him.

"He's a really nice guy. You're just over reacting. You're - too sensitive."

She tries to calm me down and make me sound like I'm a retard. He isn't nice. Not nice at all! She doesn't know how ill-mannered he is. He doesn't respect other's feelings. He doesn't give a shit about girls.

"Okay, I understand." I finally say. I don't want Chloe to think I'm crazy acting like shit for a never mind.

Actually, it isn't only because of that. I've reason to hate him. A whole lot of them. He thinks he can get any girl? Like hell no! He would never get ANY girl. Daisy is such a nice girl and I see no reason for her getting dumped by a stupid psychopath.

I'm going insane. I hate him so much. Why do I hate him? Is it only because of Daisy?

I've never acted this way over a friend's broken heart. Why do I get so annoyed by him? Is it because I think he somehow liked me?

NO! Never! A guy like him! Ew! Someone who doesn't care about other's feelings at all? I would never want to date a guy like that. The thought itself brings me goose bumps. I hate goose bumps, I hate him. It's pretty clear now.

Why do I keep thinking about him though? Do I know him? Did we go to the same school before? No way. So not happening. We are from different states, we can't be studying somewhere near. We can't have any connection.

"Hey" Nathan comes to sit next to me. It's time to stop thinking about that annoying guy. I smile at him and look at the wall clock to check the time. It's been one hour already. I need to go home soon.

"Tired, huh?" Nathan adds looking at me.

"Not really. Well kind of." I'm not sure what I'm saying. I'm just too exhausted tonight. I don't care about what he thinks about me and my answers. He is a nice guy and he cares about girl's a lot. I wonder if he has a girlfriend, she must be lucky.

"You never give a straight answer though." He chuckles.

"Maybe" I raise my eyebrow at him as I see Dylan on the other side going through his phone, I try to stay focused with Nathan's comment and I softly add, "I'm just never sure about a few things."

"Oh. Do you want a drive home? If you are planning to go back?" he offers.

"Thank you, but I brought my car today." I try to sound as polite and honest as I can.

"I'm sorry." I apologize thinking maybe I should since I declined his pride.

"No you don't need to be! It's totally fine. I just didn't want to see a girl walking back home alone at night." He says.

I'm one of those girls who always walk back home alone though and when I finally have my car, I meet someone nice to help me. So happening, I sarcastically whine in my thoughts.

I smile at him and we stay quiet. Well yea I'm sixteen and I still don't have a driving license. Even though I don't have a legal license I drive my car after midnight. I just want to look mature enough to do so. Mom usually does not let me drive but there are not many cops in town so it does not really matter. Everyone owns a car these days. I'll get my driving license by next week and I'm really excited. I've been driving car since I was fifteen? But that's only during weekends.

Texas is amazing though. I've known this place for all my life.

Dylan, well he is from D.C.

CHAPTER 4

Misconception

One month later...

"He is really nice though." I answer honestly.

"Yeah... Well, I've heard enough of it so." He sounds tired.

"I'm sorry. I think we should stop talking then?" I bite my lower lip. Shit, I shouldn't have said that.

"If you want to because I think I was right about that guy before everything started? You just have this thing for him you won't stop mentioning about." He tries to calm himself down. I can hear it from his voice. He is annoyed. After all, he is a human. Of course, he would want me to be with him rather than falling in love with some Dylan guy I have no clue of.

"I think that's the only way out then." I try to end our video call by almost pressing the 'end' button but he does it first.

He is mad at me but who cares? I don't. I'm over him already now. We made a promise that we would talk to each other and be friends until we find someone we can love more than the other. That was one of the shittiest promise I've ever made in my entire life to someone I loved. I swear to god if I was someone else

I would definitely laugh at the girl thinking she is psychotic. And that other girl would be me in this case.

We should've never made such promises, it wouldn't hurt so much to let go after all he knows about me.

He was one of the most charming people at the same time. He never lied to me. He would be at his home the entire day skyping with me during weekends and texting every day after he's done with school. I can never find a guy like him for myself. Never. I would die to be with him after ten years, but now? It's just not the right time. We need to be free from one another and live our teenage life like we want to, without one another. I knew that he will be a perfect boyfriend when we're older and more mature but just not now.

I don't need him now, he doesn't need me either. We've made it all clear during our breakup and I have to get over him fully. We've made our decisions that one day if I ever drop by near his place, I will call him up and meet him. Even though I don't want to after everything we had but I still... want to. If I'm ever somewhere close to him? I want to talk to him and hug him for what I've been longing for every time while we were dating and trying to work with our distance relationship.

But why recall something that's already finished and mentioned about over and over? We're done.

We've made our decisions.

"Good that you broke up with that guy" I've heard about Grace's break up with Blake. He wasn't worth her. I park the car and slightly smile at my little sister who is no longer little now. Mom left home again today.

She jumps out of the car and leans into the passenger window and says roughly, "Well that's what you wanted."

No. I didn't want that.

She walks away fast leaving me there in my car making me feel guilty for what I said. I should've said something better. She probably cried a lot the last couple of days. I feel bad for her. She deserves someone better than that guy. I have to make her feel better. I have to make a move.

I grab my keys, my school bag and run to catch up with my sister. This is going to be so bad.

"Grace!" I call out her name. She ignores me. Wow great! Now I need to apologies her.

"Hey, I'm sorry okay?" I want her to talk to me.

"I can't accept it." We open the main entrance door and get in together for the first time in ages.

"What?" I'm surprised. She'd never let me down. "You... can't?" I slammer. Shit. I've never been so embarrassed this way in front of my sister.

"You wanted me to break up with him. Please don't play innocent with me." she snaps.

"I'm not, grace!"

"Oh! Don't tell me that you didn't take it in a different way like I'm dating guys of your age or something." She's just way too young to be that smart. How can someone figure out everything so easily?

"I just wanted you to be happy" I stop walking and grab her arms.

"He made me happy, Stella." She turns around slowly and her eyes are bloodshot. I didn't want to see her cry.

"Why'd you break up, then?" I'm so stupid to ask that. She's never going to answer me. I try to wipe her tears off by both of my thumb. That's what big sisters do, don't they? It's something that I've never done before today. I love her. I really do. It might take ages for her to understand this but I don't care anymore. She is my only sister.

"He was cheating on me." I didn't expect her to answer me but she did and it makes me so happy that she opened up to me. For a second it felt like she trusted me enough to tell me about it.

"I'm so sorry, Grace. We can talk about it after school if you want to." More like a request to her. I think she wants to talk. She nods. That's what I wanted my little sister to do. I smile at her and we bid our good byes.

I've been thinking about her the entire day.

After school when I'm walking with Emma she then interrupts our silence, "Hey, what's going on? Are you worried about something? It seems like you're thinking too much."

"I'm not worried. I'm just thinking about Grace." I sadly add then, "She's been going through so much lately and I'm really happy that she told me the reason for her beak up."

"She was dating Blake, right? I heard about them. Everyone knew that this was coming. "She slowly pats on my back. She's right. Everyone in school knows how screwed up Blake is. He and his ego. Even though he is a great singer, it doesn't mean that he can go breaking hearts of all the girls and this is about my sister now.

We go to our locker and we walk down the stairs. Then I see Dylan. Lately, I've been talking to him. I smile at him and so does he. I don't really talk to him in school because I feel uncomfortable. After we cross by him Emma winks at me and giggles. I smile at her and then I see that girl Emma somehow knows.

They say hi to each other right when Chloe joins us. Chloe and I start talking about our English class. I didn't realize that Emma was listening to us quietly. Then Chloe asks Emma, "You know that girl?" Right after that girl leaves.

"Yeah, I do." She slightly smiles while I'm drinking my water ignoring her answer.

"I don't like her. The way she looks at me is creepy. I feel like she talks about me." Chloe softly says, trying not to let anyone else hear what she just said.

I and Emma giggle together. Our smile fades away as soon as I see my sister standing right in front of me.

"I'll go home by myself." She says out loudly and leaves us there standing all startled. I don't know what to say or how to react. She just saw me laughing when she is feeling down, when she needed someone to talk to.

"Chloe... Move over next to Jonathan"

"Stella, move over to the seat next to Dave."

"Jennifer next to Shane."

"Daisy, well next to Andrea"

I turn around to see who Dave is. Then I see an arm moving, telling me that I have to sit there. So that's Dave. Looks fine, hope he doesn't annoy me like my last seat mate. He smiles at me when I grab my chair next to him. We exchange our information and the courses we take this semester. He seems like a very nice and understanding guy to me.

After class during lunch break everyone's complaining about their seat partner except me. Especially Chloe, poor her, she was chosen first to sit next to Jonathan. She doesn't want to sit next to him. Probably because she likes him.

Chloe asks me about my seatmate.

"He's a cool guy. I like him." Well, I'm glad my seat partner is Dave, unlike Chloe sitting next to her crush. I just can't stop laughing at her. I would freak out if I sit with my crush and I think that crush would be Dylan.

Dylan. I haven't seen him for a few days.

The last time I talked to him was around four days back? When we smiled at each other? Not even talk more like a gesture. Why didn't I see him, though? Is he sick? Did he go somewhere with his family or something? How is he doing? Hope he is fine. I'm just over-reacting. He should be fine. He is.

We have our lunch and head back to our classes.

Empty class. Oh yeah. We were supposed to have a half day today. I'm so stupid. How could I not even remember that? I'm sure the girls and the gang are planning some shitty idea to scare me off anytime soon. They were just behind me five minutes back until I started thinking about Dylan again.

He is trouble.

Now when I don't want to walk through the classroom door and get pissed at my friends for pushing me inside and scaring the hell out of me, I'm staring at my phone. Dylan's last message, "See you, then" which was sent six days back and oh my goodness I miss him.

As I slowly walk by the class room door, I hear voices screaming at me and I can feel someone's harsh touch on my back. Of course my friends are trying to scare me but I'm more pissed off than scared.

"What the hell, guys?" I scream at them from the top of my lungs.

"Hey, relax."

"How am I supposed to relax? When for four days I haven't even seen -" I turn around to see the last person I wanted to see when spitting out my thoughts, but I was happy too for some reasons, Dylan's best friend who apparently is my seatmate. My eyes widen. Shit. I sigh and end up with, "Hi, Dave."

I didn't even know that I've held in so much air within. He says his hi and smiles awkwardly at me showing his rabbit teeth like my day couldn't get any worse. I look around getting totally distracted by my annoying friends behind me. I get disappointed then, I don't see Dylan anywhere. Where the hell is he?

The girls laugh and I follow them to one of the classrooms.

"It'll just take ten minutes." Chloe reminds us, for the fifth time in a minute. She has to ask some questions to her teacher. I didn't pay attention for which subject and all. I usually leave out the details.

As we enter the class we grab some chairs and take our seats because we are all just too tired with all that scaring me shit and there I see Dave walking in with a bright smile. I smile at him, remembering how I reacted at him earlier and as my eyes follow him, I see Dylan. He was in the class, around the corner we weren't facing. I don't like him.

His smile doesn't make my heart flutter. Seeing him did not make me happy. It rather made me mad and angry since I didn't have any idea where he was for few days, but now that I do, I don't want to see him. I don't look at him the entire ten minutes Chloe promised and the time's just passing by. He is here in the same class as me for about only the second time since I entered this school.

I just want to leave now. I know that I don't love him. I would never fall in love with a guy I don't have any clue about and what so ever this Dylan guy is just a misconception nothing more.

I look at him and I see him laughing with a girl sitting next to him.

"You know Dylan?" Chloe pulls her chair closer to mine.

"No." Yes, I do. I think I like him, but I'm not sure. Do you like him too? If I tell her the truth am I going to ask her this? I'm sure she doesn't or maybe she does. She has been in this school longer than I have. She probably knows everyone here present in this class, including Dylan and that girl with him too.

"He's kind of cute, don't you think?" I see my assumption, unfortunately coming out to be true. She likes him.

"I don't know." I almost whisper.

"You know he is that kind of guy who thinks he can get any girl. I just hate him." Thank god she does. I would feel horrible if not.

"He seems nice, though." I smile at her.

"Trust me when I say this, his ego and that attitude he carries are so hateful toward girls. He is really arrogant too. He just wants the girls to fall for him and when they do he won't give a shit." I've at least figured that out by now.

"Okay." I don't look at her. I keep on staring at him. Is it right, Dylan? Is she telling the truth? I want to ask him, but I can't. Every part of me says she is right, but some part says I am.

Well, she might be right though. He is ignoring me and Chloe is a reliable person. So, it's a misconception indeed.

CHAPTER 5

Mixed feelings

"Why do you even like him?" Chloe finally breaks in. I've been hiding my feelings for about two months now from her, Dave, Sydney, Andrea and everyone else I know. The only person I've talked about Dylan would be Emma. I knew that Chloe would react this way, one of the reasons I didn't want to tell her until I get over Dylan. Yes, I want to get over Dylan. He is nowhere good according to my friends and I know my friends are right about him. Even though if I don't accept it, I somehow know that they are right.

"Shit, since when?" Chloe asks me again as I didn't answer her last question. I shouldn't have said anything to her in the first place.

Thinking of it, when did I first start liking him, though? Maybe after seeing him at Jonathan's place. Yeah, that's probably when I first started having feelings for him, I suppose if I'm not mistaken.

"About two months back." I don't want to give her all the details like when, how and why because that's something I haven't yet figured out. Why did I like him? And how? He's been a good friend to me recently even though I don't consider him as just friend. I look at him as a man and that's something he probably knows better than I do.

"And you didn't bother telling me?" Chloe asks another question again. I don't want to play this question answer game right now. Especially when she just reminded me of the first time when I actually fell for that Dylan guy if I'm right about it. I'm not going to Jonathan's place from now on.

"I need to go home." I ignore her question and I get into my car which is just a few minutes far from my sight. I close the door and sigh. I'm so awful. I just acted like one of those mean girls. The one's I have always hated. I like someone who dumped my best friend just a few months back and I'm so retarded to hide it from her. I have to tell Daisy about it someday, but I'm not sure if I can. What will she think about me? A boyfriend stealer? Well, they weren't dating so apparently it would be just a boy stealer.

I pull my school bag and try to leave her house as soon as I can. I don't want to listen to any of the bullshit that I know Chloe's going to lecture me about. I wanted to study with her, but I just ended up telling her about what I feel for Dylan like what the actual Shit was I thinking? Am I in my right mind? Dylan? Hell no! No way! Not at all!

I should really stop thinking about him.

"Stella!" Chloe calls my name rushing out from her room. Shit. I was waiting for it.

"Like I told you before, he is not the kind of guy you see him as."

"What do you even know about him?" I finally turn around to see her face even though I didn't want to but I need an explanation. I actually need reasons to not like him, a lot of them.

"He's arrogant, selfish, mean, and carefree. What more do you want to hear?" She walks towards me.

"Tell me something that I don't know." I raise my eyebrows because that's something I've known about him even before talking to him. I want to know why she doesn't like him. Why is he not worth the feelings I have for him according to Chloe? What did he do to her?

Did he dump her too?

"I've seen him not picking up the books someone dropped right in front of his feet. I've seen the look he gives at other girls when they bump into him by mistake. "She sighs.

"Okay?" I ask her sarcastically folding my arms. She makes no sense telling me this stuff when I needed to hear something else.

"It's the look that says you like me, but I don't like you. You did it on purpose and I know it, but I don't give a Shit." She sounds about right. I think I've actually seen that look on him. I've seen it once or twice or maybe more.

That's the look he gave me the first time I saw him staring at me and probably every time after that day.

Those eyes I found mysterious about. The ones I fell for. The ones that make me think hard about what he might be thinking when I find him looking at me. I thought they were in admiration, but they are actually false accusation.

He thinks I like him.

As I sit next to Dave in my History class, I try my best not to let him know about Dylan. He's been asking me for days now about who I like. How will he react when he comes to find out that I like his best friend? He always asks about the guy I like every time he gets bored. He doesn't like history, but I do. I want to pay attention to the teacher and be a good student, but he keeps on distracting me. I'm sure as hell that he'll ask me about it again.

"Stella." he whispers. Oh sure, I was just looking forward to it.

"Yeah?" I whisper too without facing towards him and pretending like I'm listening to the teacher. After a while he passes me a paper, a letter to be specific.

He is talking about a friend. One of his friends and a girl. I can't quite make out his handwriting, but it's about his friend and a girl who likes him.

"What about it?" I ask him.

"I don't know what to do. What should I tell him because he came to ask me about her and I felt really bad about it" I didn't expect him to open up so much to me but I'm happy knowing that he is actually trusting me on this. He probably wants my opinion on this.

"Tell him the fact. How you think the kind of person she is. Doesn't answering him come naturally as a friend? Why did you feel bad anyway?"

"I used to like her." He sounds hurt to me. Anyone would.

"So does he-" I try to ask him when he answers me before completing my sentence.

"He knows it, that's why he was asking me about her." Scratch hurt, he is way too hurt that his friend didn't think much about it. That guy is really screwed up like seriously. Who does that? Wait, who is he?

"Um... Dave? Who's that friend of yours?" I don't whisper this time because we've been whispering for a while now and it has been really tiring.

"You probably know him." I look at him with the 'I have no idea' face and he gets me easily. We are really good at communicating and he finally says something which is the last thing I wanted to hear.

"It's Dylan." He finally spits out his name. Why Dylan? Why? I don't know what more I can say about him.

"What?!" I don't even know how I am even able to speak after having too much shock in one minute.

"Stella and Dave if you peep could be quite for a moment and watch the documentary it might be very useful for your final test that's coming up next week."

"I'm sorry" we say in unison and I'm speechless for the rest of the class thinking about Dylan. Everything Dave told me about the girl and that guy... Dylan. Dylan really went to Dave for his suggestion? Like seriously, who would do that? I can't think of anything worse than this now.

"What kind of a person is she?" I finally ask Dave, whispering again in the last five minutes of class.

"Mean, very mean. Nice at first, but she usually goes for popular guys and I don't know why Dylan doesn't get it." He probably doesn't want to.

"What's her name?"

"Madeline. Do you know her? She is really pretty, has long hair, junior." The way he said that she is really pretty strikes me hard. What if she is? I would feel so awkward liking Dylan when he has his own love story going on with someone way prettier than me. I hate this feeling.

"I don't know her, yet. I'll probably find out who she is by tomorrow." I'll either ask about this Madeline girl to Chloe or anyone else I know. During the lunch break, I tell Chloe everything that just happened.

"So what are you going to tell him once you see Madeline? Because I've seen her several times and she is quite pretty according to me."

"I'm not sure." I answer her honestly. I don't know what to do once I see her. How will I feel after seeing her? I'll probably feel hurt inside.

"Are you going to tell Dave that you like Dylan? Wait... are you in love with Dylan? If so, do you actually want to date him?" She finally asks me tons of questions. I know that she's been dying to hear it out from me about him. I slowly grab my wallet to go buy lunch for me and I turn around to Chloe again. I can see her puzzled face like crystal clear.

"I don't know what I want, so don't ask me because I'm still trying to figure it out." I use one of my favorite lines and now that it actually makes a lot of sense to me I think I'll use it more often.

I wink at her, a playful wink and I can see her smile broadening.

She softly nods going the other way to get some Italian food.

"Oh my god!" I yell after banging into someone on the way to my third period class right after lunch.

"I'm so sorry, Stella. Are you okay?" I hear a familiar voice which is very calm and friendly at the same time. I pick up my Math textbook and smile at him reassuring him that I'm totally fine.

It's Nathan. Thank goodness. I actually needed his help to ask something which is very important to me at the moment.

I lean closer to his ears as he hesitates, probably thinking that I'm going to kiss him or some shit. I cover my mouth with my right hand preventing not to let anyone around us hear what I'm going to mumble.

"Do you know a girl named, Madeline?"

CHAPTER 6

Nobody loves anyone

"Awww come on!!! It's been like forever since we last met anyone!" Chloe cries.

"I'll try." I finally tell her, whispering.

I drop her at her place which is fifteen minutes from my house. As I park my car in the garage, I hear voices, familiar ones from my house, from second floor where mom's room is. Its mom and dad. I franticly jog to the room I haven't been to for ages just to see my dad.

As soon as I reach by the door, I hear them yelling from the top of their lungs. Are they nuts? The neighbors might call the police! I finally step my feet inside this big room after five unbearable years. I want them to be quiet and I want to see him, my dad.

"Are you really kidding me? Please just leave for the love of god." I hear my mom yell, actually I see her. She is standing in front of the window. Her eyes are bloodshot, she's been crying but I don't give a Shit about that after everything she did to me.

"I will, once I get to leave with her. I want to be with her as a father. I want to see her grow up and you never take my calls, I'm forced to come here!" I hear his voice, my daddy. He came to get me from this horrific house. I don't see him from where I'm standing, but I can hear his voice, the same deep voice.

"You can't take her away from me!" Mom screams again. What? I'm shocked by her statement. She's never been a good mother to me and she wants to keep me away from my dad? Or is she doing this just to make my dad feel bad and lonely?

"If Stella comes to know about this, she'll be left heartbroken." Mom adds. She isn't even my mom anymore. How could she even lie so much? Wait, am I missing something?

"I'll come to the lawyer as soon as possible. I'm taking -" I could picture myself with him again.

I smile. He's finally taking me to live with him. I'd die to be with him. He came back for me, only me.

"-Grace." He finally finishes his sentence. My smile fades away. The room is still and for the most part, I'm actually falling on my knees with my heart sinking deep inside. I can hardly breathe. Tears crawl down slowly from my cheeks and I can't stop it. I cover my mouth with my hands so that I don't distract my parents. I slowly stand up to my feet as I hear my dad's footstep coming in my direction. I move to my right and hide behind the door.

I keep my one hand on the door knob and the other on my mouth. I stand still without breathing witnessing my dad from the back, going downstairs. He is leaving, again. I never got to say goodbye to him, five years back as well when he found out about the mom's affair with one of my dad's colleagues.

He left in the middle of the night without bidding me bye. I'm tired of waiting now, I feel helpless. This threatening silence will kill me alive. Suddenly the urge to breathe strikes me and I remove my hand from my mouth to breathe again.

The next second I hear the main door 'bang', my heart sinks a little deeper. I just wanted to look into his eye and say goodbye, nothing else.

I hear mom crying inside like a little child, moaning as if someone close to her just died. It's the same cry, the same one that I heard from her room five years back. I see history repeating. This is karma.

If she only hadn't let things fall off her hand because of that man, we wouldn't be seeing this day.

I try to walk down the stairs to my room, but even my legs deny my wish, it trembles and I can see goosebumps all over my bare skin that I nearly think that I didn't wear any shorts. For a second I hear nothing but mom's cry. Something I don't want to feel pity for. She's someone I don't feel sorry for anymore. Dad left because of her, Grace faces shame every time people ask her about her sheriff dad, and I don't feel anything and our family? We don't have a family.

It's all her fault, all of it.

"Are you coming?" Chloe asks me again as soon as I take the call. So many things are going on. I don't know what to do. I'll get all drunk if I go with her. I know that I won't be able to handle myself, not tonight. I literally just saw my dad and mom yelling at each other for... Grace. They both want's Grace. It's all that matters to them. They don't give a shit about me and my presence, existence actually.

"Are you coming or not?" Chloe sighs.

"Yeah, I will." I know this is going to be my worst distraction, but I'll try to work it out with it this time.

"Great! Everyone's going to be there! At ten, okay? See you then!" She hangs up. I have to admit that she sounds really excited, but I don't know about me.

It's already been one long hour and I don't see Chloe anywhere. Did she just ditch me? She forced me to come here and then she doesn't show up. She said that it's one of her friend's house. I feel so awkward being here without her,

I don't know anyone here and on the phone, she said everyone's going to be here. Who is everyone?

"Here." I see a wine glass with some ice and a lemon on top in front of my face.

Oh my god this is going to be really weird, I murmur to myself. I shake my head and turn to look at the person.

"I've had a long day." I softly try to give a reason and I see his face.

"It might help?" Dylan winks.

"What?" I slightly go blank again, not realizing what just happened.

"What about strawberries?" He smiles.

"Honestly, I like all kinds of cocktails" I slightly remark at his taste taking the glass from him.

"Actually, I've been sitting there for the last 30 minutes and you aren't moving an inch. So-"

"Why not flirt a bit with that chick?" I complete his sentence if I'm not wrong.

We laugh together. I was right. He looks much better when he is actually laughing. I mean it's my first time seeing him laugh. I've only seen him smiling once or twice.

"You're not any random chick to me, though. We've known each other for a couple of months now." He reminds me, he remembers.

"Well." I look away and watch three girls getting drunk and screaming over some vodka. Our smiles turn into a stranger laugh. I didn't realize that we were actually smiling by ourselves. We watch them for about half an hour and he seems to really enjoy it. As I turn to take a sip, I see him laughing with those rabbit teeth.

You don't have any right to be that perfect, do you? I ask him in my thoughts, vaguely smiling.

What would I do without your smart mouth?
Drawing me in, and you kicking me out
You've got my head spinning, no kidding, I can't pin you down
What's going on in that beautiful mind?
I'm on your magical mystery ride

John Legend's 'all of me' start playing and our laugh slowly switches back to smiles again, the song makes a lot of sense to us. It somehow relates to us. I don't know how or where or which line, but it does and both of us are aware of that.

"Cops are coming!" "Everyone hide!" "Hide!" People start screaming. The lights go off, but the colorful ones are still on, people start hiding glasses and bottles, cigarettes and pots. I don't see anything clearly but all I hear is noise and people rushing to different rooms of the house. Why are the cops coming? And why should we even hide?

The next second I feel someone grabbing my hand and taking me somewhere. I don't know where but I move along with it. I go where it's taking me. As we are all panicking within, I realize that the song is still playing in the background.

Cause all of me
Loves all of you
Love your curves and all your edges
All your perfect imperfections

This song is pretty much calming people down at the moment, the only tranquility in the house. I am forgetting something, Dylan. I'm forgetting Dylan. Where is he?

"Dylan... I- I need to find him. "I tell the anonymous shadow like a person who is holding my wrist tightly.

"Hey, I am Dylan." He takes me to a room and I'm left off-guard when he pulls me in closer to him.

"What's happening? Why are we-? Cops? I don't get it." My curious mind speaks up.

"They said someone called the cops mentioning about drugs and all."

"But they'll find us." My concerned and uptight self takes over.

"That's why we stay where we are, okay?" He almost whispers, looking into my eye. Even though in this dim room where the only light is passing through the window, I see him. I'm glad that I'm actually with him. I feel less insecure and more comfortable. He makes me feel less scared, less nervous, and less unhappy.

"Okay" I whisper. The gap between us is so less that we could hear anything from one another in a whisper; we could hear each other breathing heavily. His heart beat is much calmer than mine, but the silence in this room is actually very warm. He is very warm, like the first time I saw him next to the locker. I saw a warm and nice person standing there. That's who he is. Not the guy who my friends talk about, not the one they say is mean. This guy in front of me is the one I first saw him as, and I know that I'm absolutely right. I love him since I know him.

The song is still playing and it's probably starting to annoy everyone hiding in different rooms. I softly giggle and Dylan loosens his grip to let me go. I don't want him to but once he does, we both leave out a long breathe we weren't aware of.

The door slowly cracks open and we see some shadows walking in. The cops. We need to run. This time, I take his wrists and take few steps towards the window. I don't know why, perhaps to jump? But he shakes his hand just to let him go off from mine and out of all this chaos. I'm hurt by his, this one move. I'm left with utter confusion by his reaction.

"April Fools!" The shadows start's screaming. Sure. How did I even forget about it? It's 31st of March. I'm such an idiot. Out of all day I had to be with Dylan, today? He was just fooling around, for the whole time. Everything was just a joke.

The lights are turned on and I see every one of my friends not any cops. Chloe hugs me and laughs like a mad man with all the others, Emma, Jake, Sydney, Nathan, Daisy, Blake who is my sister's ex. And Dylan.

"They said no one could ever fool you during April fools. So I just tried and accomplished. "Dylan explains himself with that smile I just fell in love with, just an hour back.

Why do you make me feel betrayed? Why do I feel like you are not trustworthy anymore? Why did I even believe you at first place? I should have known that you were just being yourself. Trying to win over girls, always trying to prove something about you.

"That was ridiculous" I tell them with my conscious mind and serious face.

I know I was unconscious while believing everything that Dylan said to me.

I push everyone to get a way for me to leave the house, but as I start moving, I see Dylan's guiltless face. The face I'm starting to hate once again and this time I'll make it the last time.

> *Poetry in motion, put it right there*
> *Deeper than skin, crystal clear*
> *Letters don't fade, titanium made*
> *Forever here, forever saved*

Selena Gomez's 'Write your name' plays right after I walk past the group. And as I walk down the road all I can think of is Dylan, his eyes, his face, his arms, his smile, his laugh, his dirty trick, back stabbing, deception and every other word that's near to betrayal ends up with him.

"Are you leaving?" Emma asks as soon as I take her call.

"I already left." I hang up on her. All of my friends pulled a prank on me. Despite knowing the fact that I have feelings for Dylan, especially Emma and Chloe. They did this on purpose, didn't they? I feel more shattered and hurt.

I play a song once I reach my car and the first song that plays, strikes me.

> *What would I do without your smart mouth?*
> *Drawing me in and you kicking me out*
> *You've got my head spinning, no kidding, I can't pin you down*
> *What's going on in that beautiful mind?*
> *I'm on your magical mystery ride*

It makes more sense now than ever. I was too vulnerable to understand anything earlier next to Dylan. I should have never trusted him.

Actually, I won't ever trust him again.

Something that Chris Isaac said, "Nobody loves no one. Nobody" I whisper to myself with all the tears that had been struggling to fall. I cry over and over again for what my life has become. I couldn't go to my own home because no one cares and now when I needed my friends, they pull a damn prank on me!

It's been the worst day of my life.

CHAPTER 7

Liking that person

I park my car and remember the scene I witnessed earlier in the same spot, excitedly rushing toward mom's room and forgetting everything behind me just to see that man I have dearly loved and cherished all my life.

"Dad was here" My sister reminds me from the door.

"I know." I step inside and she follows me closing the door.

"He's taking one of us with him." My sister informs me, she thinks I don't know.

"You." I snap at her.

"Mom's hoping to see you in her room." She tries to hide away her guilt and pity she has towards me, but I at least know that face of her by now.

"I don't care." Mom's been acting like a freak lying to dad about me and I actually don't care about her at all right now.

"Then what do you care about?" She steps forward, impulsively.

"Silence." I am honest. I need silence right now. Only silence and not her.

I take a step forward and she grabs my wrists, reminding me of how Dylan did few hours back in the party when the lights went off.

"You.. You won't ever change, will you?" She slammers and then she pressurizes her fist tighter only to hurt me but I don't know what to feel bad for at the moment. I feel so heartless. Every part of me is already into hundreds of pieces since this afternoon. One by one, all the people who are dearest to me made me feel down and I just don't know what to feel bad for anymore.

"Do you even remember what kind of a person I was like at first?" I ask her without answering because I sure as hell know that she doesn't have an answer for that.

"Yeah, I do." Her answer takes me by surprise as I finally raise my eyes to look at her, my half- sister.

"You were a very caring, loving, smart, spontaneous, funny, warm, and honest and an amazing sister," she adds and it almost fills up my eyes but I hold in my tears and I gulp a very strong pain down my neck.

"But.. you were. Now I don't even know who you are." She ends it with a very sentimental sentence which I fall for.

You know me Grace, more than anyone else in my life. You know me well enough. Her eyes are bloodshot and I can't do shit to stop it. I feel hopeless and for the most part, broken by each and every word anyone has said to me today.

I slowly try to walk past her but then something holds me in there with her. I didn't even realize that she's still holding my wrists. I try to shake off my hands from hers, but she only grips it more and more tightly every time.

"You should really forget about that guy you like. I've heard a few things about him. A lot actually."

"Oh yeah? Tell me about it." I never imagined that I would get to hear this from my sister, relationship advice? That's some screwed up shit to hear from her.

"He's just not your type." She comes up with something positive rather than all the thousands of other negative things about him that I already know. I agree with her, though. I totally agree with her about my type. He is not my type, not even close to one.

She leaves the living room, letting be here all by myself to think about him, all over again. Something that I have been doing for the past couple of days and I clearly don't have any idea how long it's going to take for me to get over this feeling.

A week later...

"Pleaseeeee come with us!! Just for tomorrow... I swear nothing like the last time that happened between you and Dylan will ever happen again." Chloe begs again for the tenth time today.

Dylan... it feels like forever since I last heard his name.

"Thanks but I really don't want to go this time. I'm really tired and I have lots of assignments to finish."

"Geez, you're smart as hell. You can finish them in less than an hour. Don't pretend, okay?" Sydney adds and it just makes me feel grounded among my friends. I can never get to breathe some fresh air without them. I don't hate them but I just don't want to get stuck or get attached to everything they do, eat, talk or laugh at in those house parties. Especially when I'm going through a lot of things these past few weeks.

"Shit, look at that guy. I think I have to break up with my annoying boyfriend, right away." Sydney changes the topic looking at a guy who is actually not bad.

"But it would be really weird breaking up after two weeks... I mean... If I at least make it last for three, it would be better right?" Sydney adds and turns around to look at us for an answer just to find all of us giving the 'wow' look at her.

"What?"

"You're so weird, like seriously." Emma answers and the rest of totally agree with her and we nod.

"What? Three isn't better? Okay. Three and a half, then?"

We all laugh at her and then I see him looking at me. He didn't even apologize for that night. Even though, I know that he won't but I just don't want it to be true. I want him to tell me that he is sorry for how he made me feel. He, it's never going to happen anyways. I don't need to think much about it.

Dylan.. I softly whisper to myself. I really believed everything you said that night.

"Babe.." Emma whispers softly in my ears from behind.

"He was staring at you."

She pinches my belly and I smile at her. She knows me better. She knows that I actually really like him and I can't change that.

"I hate him." I look away and look at her just to let her know that I'm not lying which I'm not.

"But deep inside your feelings are fighting for him. I know the feeling, I've had it too." Once she mentions about her, I then realize that the things happening to me are exactly what she went through and all this only ends up to one of those bad heartbreaking story.

"I'm sorry, Emma." I really feel bad for her and how things went wrong with her.

"Have you ever loved someone so much that it almost kills you to not see them every day?"

She takes me by surprise with her question. Why would she ask this? That too all of a sudden?

"Yes." I reply honestly, I always have.

"Dylan's that guy, right?" Too much shock in five seconds.

"Huh?" I don't know what to say.

"He makes you feel horrible?" She looks at me with those eyes full of trust and care.

I nod; I can't even speak a word about him anymore. Thoughts about him start crawling on my mind and it just drives me crazy.

"You sound like a professional love guru." I wink at her and she giggles.

"You already know." She says with a British accent making us laugh harder by ourselves as Chloe, Sydney and Andrea gives us this weird look.

"Hey, Stella!" he makes his way through the crowd jogging towards me while I try my best to ignore and not to make eye contact with him.

I look at him just for one second and I actually examine him very well. He is wearing his dark jeans matching with his dark blue bag and he looks good as always.

"Um... can I talk to you...? Just for few seconds?" he takes me by surprise with his question. I smile to myself deep inside, a feeling that only I will know at the moment and I don't want to ever feel this way for someone else.

"Sure."

"I want you to talk to me. It's been over a week already, I'm sorry." He looks into my eye and I look away. He can be really nice but at times it just makes me feel horrible. Emma was right, he makes me feel horrible.

"Sure, we can but just tell me when this is done. When you get tired of me talking to you."

"And that day will never come." He smiles. How can you manage to smile? After making me go through hell that night, he smiles... just like that. Like.. Nothing happened.

"I hope so but we're never sure about that, are we?" I try to make it sound as short and as accurate as I can to make him understand what I'm thinking.

"Yeah.. well. That's the other thing and I will tell you." so easy for you, Dylan? So easy to tell a girl that you're tired of her? I don't even know why I still like him.

"Sometimes, I wish I didn't see you." That day next to the locker. I wish I knew that this would be coming if I see you.

"What?"

"Nothing" I shake my head and he doesn't bother to ask me about it even once.

As I take a bite from my apple doing my Math assignment, there's a knock at my door.

"It's open."

The door creaks and as I tilt my head towards the door and look back at my book, I realize the person standing there next to the door... Mom.

I try my best not to look at her again as she drags her feet towards me, coming closer in each step making my skin crawl all over making me nervous.

It's like an old scar getting scratched by her presence.

"Stella, I wanted to talk to you.. Honey, I don't want to be a burden for you."

"You aren't." I snap at her, I want her to leave, but she should know that she isn't. I feel like I am a burden to her.

"That's... good to hear." Her voice gets thicker as it cracks in between making it obvious that she is almost about to tear up.

"What brings you here?" I slightly want to know why she actually came in and why she lied to dad and why dad doesn't want me... but.. I just want to know why he didn't come to see me for all these years.

"I heard you broke up with that distance guy and the guy you like now... he-"

"Mom, please. Save it."

"Stella, I know I have no right to interfere in your personal life according to your thinking but for me? It's the only possible way to be a small part in your life and that would make me really happy."

"I'm not in a mood for a mother-daughter bonding."

"I know what you're going through. It was the same with me." I slightly get interested in the last word. She is trying to relate my life with her. She finds us similar? Our situations, probably?

"When I first met your father we were teenagers and I never expected to be with anybody else, never. But then one day things changed and it's over. And I'd be lying if I tell you that it still doesn't hurt, it does but honey it's like a broken bone that healed and it still throbs every time it's rubbed against something hard." She gives her speech crying.

"We have nothing in common, mom." My eyes fill up with tears that never wanted to show up next to my mom.

"We have nothing in common" I repeat myself.

"I promise this is going to go away. This feeling, you will get over it. You'll find someone who will actually make you smile for who you are and I know that day isn't far enough if you wait for a little while." She tries to console me but it doesn't work, nothing works and nothing is going to work to ease my pain.

It's not only about him, it's about dad and me and mom and my sister and my friends and everything, every single thing I pass through. It's just broken.

Like me.

"There will be people who will force you to leave things behind, things that mean the world to you, but you should never feel like you have nothing left because you will always have something. Something you should fight for."

"I don't know what to feel... I... Dad.. Dylan... I don't know... If anybody will ever be there for me... "I finally open up a little of me for the first time with my mom and it lifts away some burden off my chest that I was not capable of to carry.

"Honey, sometimes we feel isolated even though we are surrounded by hundreds of people we are closest to. That's when you should know that you can always come to your mom to share your heart breaks, anything that you aren't able to share to others. You can share it with me."

"I can't... just leave me alone." I cry, I cry louder.

She pats on my back and with those bloodshot eyes, she leaves the room. But all I can think of is hating my dad and Dylan.

I hate them, specially dad who never cared enough to come to see me even for a second.

I hate him with each and every cell that my body carries.

And Dylan? He's been a fake the whole time and I want to forgive and forget but I just can't. If I forgive him once he will take me as an easy going girl, if I don't? I'm going to have a very rough time trying to hate him. I just don't want him to hurt me anymore. I want this pain to go away. I can fall for someone else, it's easy. He was just not meant for me, we have nothing in common.

As I walk down the stairs with the four girls and two boys, Dave and Nathan who is going to point out Madeline for me outside the school. Meanwhile, when Emma stops by in the basketball court, she starts talking to a girl and we are talking among ourselves.

Nathan whispers, "That's her." I look around trying to find the girl Dylan would like, but I don't see his type anywhere around me and Nathan repeats again lifting his finger this time, "That's her, Melanie."

As I turn to my left looking at where Nathan just pointed and I see Emma... Emma's friend, the girl Emma talks to. I have not told Emma about Melanie yet. I don't know what's going to happen next, but this girl is totally not the girl I imagined.

Yup, she has long blonde hair, but she looks kind of rough. I can literally hear her talking to Emma about someone, which is getting on my nerves because I don't like these stuffs. Especially not when this is the girl I am supposed to despise the most.

"She's not pretty." Sydney and Emma say in unison staring at Dave's taste.

"I agree." I add to them and I totally do think that she's not that pretty, as weird as it sounds because I'm like her rival to them. But no matter what, she isn't like how Dave described to me. She is way too different than I could have ever imagined this girl to be like. Her first impression itself is not good, even though I have seen her a few times before, but this time I look at her, briefly and I don't like her at all. Dylan likes her, though, and I can't ever change that.

CHAPTER 8

Saudades for him

"Just tell him already." Chloe begs during lunch as Sydney winks with her right eye at me.

"I can't." I answer her ignoring Sydney.

"How long has it been?"

"Ten months?" I didn't realize that time actually passed so fast.

"You should really ask him out, Stell." Sydney suggests with a gossip girl look.

"I.. can't." I repeat again, just in case they didn't hear me the first time.

"I heard it the first time." Chloe pulls her chair closer to mine.

"Ten months, Stell! You must be kidding me if you think that I'm just going to watch you wait for him any longer." Sydney bursts out and drinks her water from the bottle with a serious look.

"It's too much, okay? You like him, sincerely. So, what are you afraid of?" Chloe asks looking into my eye, holding my hands now.

"But he doesn't like me-" I answer. Chloe and Sydney raise their eyebrows together telling me that I'm wrong.

"Sincerely" I finish my sentence.

"What are you afraid of, Stell?" Emma asks, placing her plate on the table and sitting beside me.

"I.. I don't know." I almost whisper and gulp.

What am I afraid of? All of my friends are asking me for what am I afraid of. What is there to not be afraid of? Literally, everything about him is to be afraid of.

"Stell.. Stell!" Emma shakes me by my shoulder.

"Yeah.. What?"

"We were asking you if you would want to come to-"

"No, I'm really tired. Seriously." I snap.

"Um.. Okay.." Emma looks sad as she turns around and I can't stand still.

"Okay." I give up.

"Okay, what?" Chloe asks.

"I will come." just for Emma's sake. I'm not going to drink or dance because I'm just not in a mood for anything joyful.

Emma shrieks with happiness hugging me tightly and I'm glad the reason for her happiness is me. It's her birthday. I can't make her upset about something so minor.

"Happy birthday, Emma." A voice from behind says and walks among us with an unexpected hug from the girl that I've been despising the most for few months now.

"Hey, Madeline! Thanks! You have to come to the party tonight." Emma pulls away from the hug.

"Sure." Madeline smiles at her and leaves the group as no one dared to utter a single word in her presence.

"Why did you invite her?" Sydney asks Emma gloomily right after the blonde leaves which actually makes me happy for her concern towards me.

"She is my friend." Emma answers coldly.

"She is your best friend." Chloe steps in front of Emma pointing at me. Making me smile for these are the reasons my friends are beyond everything else in my life. Even though getting mad at Emma isn't what I want, but them standing for me is something that I've always seen and I don't want them to change.

"I'm really sorry." Emma turns towards me joylessly.

"It's fine, Emma. She's your friend and one invitation is not going to spoil my time with him." I wink at her enthusiastically as if I am a bad girl and everyone laughs.

"Just go say hi and be like what's up?" Chloe suggests while Sydney and Emma are busy talking to the boys in Emma's other room.

"Okay, but he is with Elijah." I'm pretty sure that's his name.

"It doesn't matter! Just go say hi." Chloe pushes me like rocking a little kid further away from you to make them go to sleep; the push was neither too hard nor too soft.

I look at him and I see him standing still, looking down at his phone and I think for a few minutes about everything that has been going on with us for the past few months. He has been really sweet and he told me that I'm the only one to know so much about him, which actually makes me really glad.

The exhilarating feeling I get every time I see him is still exactly the same like the first time when I saw him following me after the party, if my assumptions are correct. My smile is so bright that anyone around me who noticed it would find out that I'm staring at the man I love the most.

I take two steps and my heart just falls on my knees. My smile fades away and as the second pass by, I'm dumbfounded. My hands are numb and I almost feel like I just saw a nightmare in the middle of a heavenly world of mine. I want to move but I can't, I want to not cry, but my eyes just fill up and tears crawl down my cheek like a dying lagoon. The feelings are shattered and crumbled in such a way that I can't feel a thing for a minute, but can only see the worse I've ever seen.

I see him... with her.

My lips slowly fall apart, but the words do not come out clearly even in my thoughts, but I manage to pull them out my vocal and as I whisper just to realize that I am conscious and what I'm seeing is for real, "Dylan is with Madeline." The word finally makes its way out and I turn around, away to not see them at all.

I make my way through the crowd and climb up the stairs to the balcony just to hide my tears from all the people I know.

"Stell..?" Emma walks toward me frightened as it's obvious that I've been crying out loud for the past ten minutes on her balcony.

"Wha- what happened?" She walks closer to look at me closely in this dark night.

"Why didn't I see her? Why didn't I see her?" I keep on blaming myself for everything that has happened to me and I am to blame, no one else.

"Tell me what happened, please. Who are you talking about? Who is her?" Emma asks impatiently as I grieve louder.

"I saw Dylan... I was going to talk to him... and then.. she was there... I.. I couldn't make it to him.. because... she was there, Em. I... Felt like I was... helpless... Like I lost to her..." I stammer, breathing hard, each and every word poking me from inside.

"I don't want to feel this way, Em. I don't want to... feel this way for anyone. I don't want to.." I keep on talking, explaining myself, not mentioning it to her about how hurt I am inside because of him. I talk in riddles but I hope maybe someday he will come to know, how much it hurts.

"How could I forget... that... he likes her... and... I'm just expecting so much from him...? When I shouldn't be." I don't know why he makes me so weak, but this is what he does to me. Emma hugs me tightly, ensuring me that she will always be there for me no matter what.

"How will I face Daisy? How am I going to hide it from her? This feeling I have for Dylan... I... have to tell her... I can't hide it any longer. She has to know and I'm sure that she'll be the one helping me out from this mess."

I hid this thing from Daisy because I was sure that I would get over Dylan in a few days, but... but it's been 10 months already now. I don't think it has ever been easy for me to like a guy like him, but Daisy is over him, she might help.

"She will figure it out, Stell but first... you shouldn't feel this way for that guy. Everybody warned you before and I'm telling you again, just try and get over him. He's not worth it; he's not worth any of this." She pulls off from the hug to look at me, for how miserable I look.

"God, Stella. I'm really worried about you. Things between you and Dylan... it's just getting over the head now and I don't know how to convince you for you to stop having this uneven feeling. Trust me when I say this, He does not deserve any of your tears." She adds. Making me feel better that she is trying her best to not make the situation any worse which already is.

"I can't forget... seeing her there. It's just like a picture to me now that's stuck in my head. Her face, she was smiling and she looked happy-" I exhale the air I've been holding in and I finally stop crying for what just happened.

Emma is right; he doesn't deserve any of my tears.

After drinking and talking with all the other girls trying to forget everything, I see Dylan walking towards me.

I don't know why I'm still happy and nervous looking at him but I just don't want to feel this way. I want to quit this feeling.

"Stella, I... I heard you just walked away from me? Earlier?" He asks me with hesitation like he never wanted to talk about it. Words always travel fast in this world.

"No... I just wanted to ask you something... but it's totally fine now." I lie. I'm not fine, not at all but you have no rights to know anything about me and my hurtful feelings for you.

"Look... I'm extremely sorry for what you saw... I swear you don't need to worry about anything as such. You can come anytime to talk to me, no matter who I am with or where I am. I will always be there for you. "His words... they make me smile but I can't smile, can I? He is lying like always. I can't trust you Dylan, can I? I keep on asking him questions deep inside but I know the answer is always going to be no. I can't trust him.

I nod at him and leave the room only to go back to the balcony again.

I open my bag and pull out my phone, go to the camera and I look at myself. My eyes are swollen and my lashes are spoilt, I actually look sick and I don't want to look this way. Why do things always happen the way I don't want them to happen at all? I fix my makeup and try to feel a bit better. I take out my earphones, unscramble them and play one of my favorite songs.

> *"Sometimes, sometimes I wonder, I wonder how people like you*
> *like people like me that like people like you"*

I eventually end up smiling after all, the worst possible things that has happened to me, I smile thinking about him. I don't want to think about him, but the more I try to hate him, the more I fall deep. I can't stop thinking about him at all, maybe that's the reason why mom always wanted to be there for me to know about my love life.

She went through all these until dad came along and he swept her off the ground and I'm their only sign of love. I wonder how they first met, how they talked, how they felt, everything.

I remember every single thing that happened the first time we talked in person. When I first talked to Dylan...

Flashback

"Hey, I just wanted to tell you that you should listen to your best friend." I tell him right before our extra class on a Tuesday afternoon.

"What? I didn't get you." He leans towards me to hear me out.

"About you and that girl, Madeline. You should talk to her, sort things out fast because your friend, Dave... he is really worried about you for some reason." A couple of weeks after Dave told me about Madeline and Dylan. I just couldn't resist giving my opinion to Dylan. Which is lying?

"Um. okay?"

"I'm sorry I shouldn't be involved in this stuff, I don't even know you but I know Dave and it's all I know. He is really worried about you and what he says will only be for your good. "I feel terrible talking to this guy I don't have any idea of but I still like him for some reasons. I just want him to date someone real soon so that I can get over this guy fast. This guy who thinks he can get any girl.

"It's okay I don't know how you came to know about all this but thanks?" We walk inside the classroom, we sit in different groups but we are still close enough to talk to one another.

"He told me." I tell him and the teacher gives a bad stare to both of us and reminds us of the rules for our extra class.

"No talking once you step inside the class." Who makes these kinds of rules anyways? It's lame.

"Oh, okay." He whispers to me ignoring the annoying classroom rule. We both giggle, not sure why. I find it funny that this Dylan guy has no clue about what I'm talking but still is acting like he does. I think he is laughing for the same reason, or he probably didn't get anything of what I just said.

His response is not enough at all to me. I mean I talk a lot once I get to know a person but then this Dylan guy talks so less, it makes me feel like he doesn't want to talk to me at all but... I don't care.

He should just go date a random girl real soon or else I might actually fall for him hard because he is just really different. Not my type at all. Probably doesn't play cards, or chess, or laughs or supports any girl. I feel like he doesn't care about people at all. He just seems so heartless. Why did Daisy fall for him anyways? I am starting to hate him already. Shit, I hate him.

Flashback ends

You make my heart, heart stop

The ending of the song brings me back to reality. A time where I knew so much about him. A time that I want to forget. I don't want to know anything about him. I've tried my best to deny and ignore the fact about my feelings for him that it almost makes me feel like I'm not a human anymore, lying all the time.

I don't want to feel hopeless anymore. I want to quit admiring him, quit loving him and I know that I will sooner or later.

But I will, someday.

CHAPTER 9

Giving up

I open my eyes in the middle of the night because of the loud noise of the construction work that has been going on in the next building. It's been four days already and I still can't sleep well because of that annoying sound.

I remove the blanket and stand on my feet, slide my phone and check the time. It's just two in the morning, I whisper to myself with my one eye shut. I'm really thirsty and there are no bottles of water in my room. I usually stack them up in my room but there's none to be seen tonight.

As I drag my feet downstairs to the hallway, I hear whispers from the hall. Someone's in the living room. It only takes me seconds to realize who the figures are that are sitting on the sofa.

Its mom and Grace.

I'm seeing her after four months now. 'Where the hell have you been?' I want to yell at her for she hasn't visited us even once in five months since she last left with dad. But I can't yell. I don't have any rights to.

"Yeah, and I have a friend who is literally into a guy who's never dated any girl! He is a nice guy, but my friend? Oh my god, she just can't hold herself from loving him! He is really weird because I feel like he likes me. It's just a feeling though. I always catch him looking at me!" Grace shares and they both laugh together. Something I haven't seen for over a year.

"Oh, poor girl! You should tell her to not like someone like that!" Mom suggests giggling. Mom really likes talking about love stuff.

"I did, mom! But she doesn't listen to me." They laugh more; it's not that funny to laugh about like this.

"Mom? What about Stella?" Grace almost whispers, looking around.

"How is she and Dylan?" She asks again.

"Sweetie, what do I say about Stell? You know she never shares much about herself, she likes being secretive. All I know is that she still likes him and it seems like she's already giving up on him."

As soon as I hear about me, I quietly return back to my room with the bottle of water from the kitchen. I don't want to hear them talk about my love life. They know nothing about it. Nothing but they still tend to act like they can judge me.

Right when I come out from the shower, I hear my phone's ringtone. I had to take a shower in the middle of the night because I couldn't sleep at all.

"Hello?" I answer sliding the phone to my right and rubbing my hair with the towel with my left hand.

"Hey, Stella. I just saw Dylan with a girl! Is it possible? I couldn't say anything because I was too shocked myself!" Isaac from the other side breathed finally. Isaac is one of my very good friends and he knows Dylan too, and any connection between me and Dylan, it just doesn't fit right.

"I'm used to Dylan surprises." I sigh and check the time, 3:45AM.

"I don't have any words to describe how bad I felt for you at that moment. I really didn't know that he was dating someone. I just thought that... Holy shit... I'm really sorry Stella but I actually want to tell you that you should get over him. He is not worth your feelings."

Those words again. He's not worth your feelings.... Those again?

I remain silent for the longest seconds of my life.

"Stell.. Don't give up on him if you really like him, but don't like him in such a way that you end up regretting in the end. "He says and I hang up the phone. Don't give up?

Now when people tell me, "Don't give up" all I do is laugh because they don't know that I'm already used to giving up. Since the time I first met Dylan, all I have done is give up and I've given up every time since.

And I'm really tired of giving up.

Sometimes we don't know who we are in love with. We try our best to figure it out, but consistently we are just in loss of words once we find out the unravelling truth. We only want to protect them and we ask for nothing in return yet we still expect them to be there in our worst. I did the same and I hope it does not let me down any further than it already has.

"I like being with him but I don't know what I should do about it because there's Madeline and I don't want to change things turning towards me." I try to express myself; it's been months since I last opened up to anyone. Deep inside me, I don't think that this is the only reason though.

"I asked for what you REALLY want, Stell."

"I want him to be in love with me, but that would be selfish... I want him to date her but that would hurt me so much. It's not like I will always care, but I think I will because this time, it's about him. So, I think knowing about him and Madeline was a sign for me to leave even though if it meant that I would get hurt." I grab my school bag closing the locker and turning towards Austin sighing.

"You spend too much time on thinking about what things mean." He looks at me with the worrisome face and lined forehead.

"Only when it's about him." I whisper as I add, "But I don't want to stay with the hope-" we slowly walk through the hallways, filled with students laughing and smiling. Lunch break.

"-Thinking that maybe... Maybe just one day, he'll miss me too." I finish my sentence right when I see the girls and I wave at them as they wave back at us.

"Dylan's here." Austin smirks and I can't help but forget everything that I just said, because right now I feel like they don't make any sense while the fact is they do.

All I need to do is push away my feeling and move forward. I don't look at his direction, but I look down at my phone and start replying to all the people I haven't yet since this morning.

Trying my very best to ignore him while he says, "See ya." taking me by surprise, but well I just ignore for another few second. I stop walking and look around, there's no one but me and Austin.

"Who was he-?"

"You." He smirks, again poking near my stomach.

"Hey! Don't do that again!" I warn him as he tickles me, making me run and laugh hard which feels like after ages. This happiness, this vibe. I missed it so much.

"See ya, babe!" He mimics Dylan.

"He didn't say babe, okay?" I punch Austin's stomach with my fist making him scream like a small puppy.

"Woah! Hold on! Some romance going on?" A familiar voice tease us from behind as we turn around to look at the person, the girls.

Chloe continues, "You guys want to join us? We are planning to skip the second half of the classes today for a movie and there's a party at one of our old school friend."

"Shit, Sure!" Oh, I was planning to spend time hanging out with Austin today.

He frowns. I promised it would only be me and him.

"Sorry guys, I forgot I actually have to go somewhere with him after school." I smile at the girls sadly.

"Its fine, you can skip some other day. Have fun, see you guys tomorrow." Emma smiles. Even though I feel really sad not going with them, but that's less than how worse, I would feel guilty of for leaving Austin behind. So I choose to play nice.

"I actually think Dylan's going to the movie too. Many are." He finally planned on telling me. For a moment I wanted to yell at Austin for informing me so late and I wanted to go back to my friends and tell them that I'm going to join them but the next second all I realize is that even if I'm there in the same movie hall with Dylan, he wouldn't give a shit about it.

I should remember that I don't want to love him. Yup, still trying.

"Nah, it's better to be with you." I smile at Austin, entering our Physics class and sitting next to him is the only way to not think about Dylan. Because Austin is just that much of a good company to have and to be with.

"Stella Hamilton." The teacher calls out my name out of the blue during the last period. I don't want to change seats.

"Yes?"

"Please be seated next to Nathan."

Not bad.

I smile at him for the 10th time today. I see him every day in the hallways and I can't help but smile because that's how nice he is.

"Do you like someone?" he takes me by surprise by his question after 15 minutes.

"Umm... Strange question from you but yea, I... think so.." I think of Dylan again and the next second I'm regretting the words I just split out. Why did I even say yes?

Dylan.

My feelings.

My yeah.

Love.

Everything.

Ugh!

"You fine?" Nathan asks me with his concerned face and I painfully smile because I'm not. I'm not anywhere to fine.

"Are you stoned?"

"No, Hell no!" I answer him really fast and I see Austin turning back to look at me.

"I'm just not comfortable right now talking about some stuff. Bad morning."

"Oh, that's okay." Nathan reassures me with a smile.

"Actually I have bad mornings too. Every time I see my mom placing an extra plate with fork and knife and an empty cup on the table for the person who is never coming back. Giving up on things that natures created just doesn't come easy on her." He says, sighing and looking back at the book.

"Oh, I'm so sorry. I didn't know that your dad-" I'm terrified by the idea of death.

"-No! No! It's not how you think it is like. My dad's not dead, they actually got divorced so yeah." He giggles. Making me sigh for how he manages to giggle. It brings a smile to the people around him because some people don't have any reason to smile anymore.

"Oh! Shit! I'm so sorry I took it the wrong- I am so sorry to hear that." I complete my apology with my hands on my mouth.

"It's really fine. You don't have to. She actually believes that he's going to come back though. I know he won't. He always does, but this time it's been five years already." Wow, that's exactly how long dad's been away for.

"That's sad." I say honestly, even though I don't want to tell him about my parents. I don't like sharing similarities with strangers. He is not really a stranger, but not close enough to know the worst and the weakest part of my life.

Well, mom must have been waiting for dad too or maybe dad has been waiting for her to call him back. But I think she gave up long time back already so that basically wouldn't really matter.

"Have you ever been in love?" His question takes me by surprise, again. Is he like a detective of some sort? Sounds like one.

"If love is setting an extra plate on the table with amazing food every day for the person who is never coming, I think I'll pass." I answer him sincerely even though I've been believing that I loved my ex's and Dylan a lot but comparing to his mom... I'm nowhere near her. I can't wait for Dylan for five years, can I? No way, I can't.

"True that." he smiles at me right when the bell rings and we bid bye to each other.

"Sup? I saw you talking to that guy." Austin winks at me right after we pack our bags.

"His family... I think we have a history."

"What history?" Austin asks curiously.

"He is the same guy who had a crush on me since grade three. He is the same guy who came up to me asking for my number in grade six and texted me about his family problems. The same guy who used to help me with my assignments during grade 8 and he is the same guy who was there sitting next to me when I first fell in love with Dylan last year... grade ten in the party."

"Wow?" He raise his eyebrows in surprise for how much I remember everything but not the biggest thing.

"He is the same Nathan. How could I not remember? Holy shit! I feel so bad for him. He told me about his mom again and I could not recognize him!"

"You could NEVER recognize him, actually." He adds to my disbelief as I look at him and shake my head.

"You guys should leave." Mrs. Cooper suggests us smiling from behind and we laugh for she probably heard everything I just said.

It's actually scary how he's been around for nine whole years and I just found out now? What was wrong with me?

C H A P T E R 1 0

The falling stones of truth

The people we let go are the people we love the most.

I say this line and Dylan is the only person who makes me repeat it again and again.

"Stella Hamilton, will you please finish reading the rest of your paragraph?" The teacher's sharp voice takes over my thoughts and I can't help but feel embarrassed for how narcissist I've turned into.

> *She didn't plan to care nor stumble or move but she cared too much, stumbled every time and fell for him. Poems and movies reminded her of him, how they jungle up in her thoughts making her think of their impossible future together. She didn't plan any of these but she couldn't stop the disastrous affection she had for him. Fighting the society and their parents, they found a way to be together that was being for one another forever and after through death through soul.*

As soon as I finish my poem like paragraph everyone applauds. I start folding my notebook and smile at the audience; this was not what I expected as no one clapped for any other speakers today.

"That was indeed marvelous. I really liked your thinking, words and expression. They sound so real and beautiful. I can't find any words to compare with yours. It's deep and meaningful. I loved it, Stella. You can take your seat now as we have only five minutes for the bell." The teacher's remark on my short paragraph sounds so good; I thank her and take my seat right after.

"Are you the Juliet or some sort?" My friends ask me once I sit which literally makes me laugh for how their thoughts are different than the other mass.

"I like your paragraph." Nathan smiles at me and I feel really awkward smiling back at him after remembering and knowing everything about him. We were in the same primary school and I didn't have any idea about that until yesterday. I'm not going to tell him that I know everything because that would only make him feel ashamed and stupid for following me around.

I try to not make any eye contact with him until the bell rings which is after three minutes.

I didn't see Dylan today and school's almost over. I don't know what's coming next in our unfortunate fate.

Did I just say fate? No fate with him. I can't have any fate for a guy like him. I walk down the hallways alone for the first time in a couple of weeks. Planned on taking my car and I actually want some peace.

Right when I reach the school entrance, I see Madeline. I try my best to not look at her like how I do to Dylan. I always feel like she's staring at me if that's not weird. Dylan probably told her everything about me, how there's a girl who likes him and he most likely laughed at it. At me.

"Hey." Chloe pats on my back from behind making it obvious that it's her, she always pats.

"You've been ditching us lately." she adds.

"No, I haven't. I'm just too tired these days; you know I have joined the tennis club at one of mom's friend. I've been practicing tennis after school." I give my excuse; even though it usually never works I hope it does.

"Is it about Dylan?" Shit. She actually figured.

"Um... I hadn't talked to Madeline for a long time now after my party and I now agree with you guys about her personality. "Emma innocently informs us about her friendship with Madeline getting worse, which doesn't make me happy but guilty and sad.

"You know you don't have to be this, right? You can talk to her and don't change your opinion on her just because of our assumptions." I smile at her trying not to force her over doing something she doesn't want to.

She remains quiet.

"I hate that girl, though." Sydney rudely remarks.

"Guys, she doesn't deserve the hate."

I snap at them and leave without wanting to hear anything else from them.

"Hey, can I get in?" Dylan bends his body over the passenger window asking me for a lift home at the lot.

"No, can't." I start my car.

I leave him there standing alone in the parking lot. After approximately one minute of my insane admiration for him I take a U-turn.

He is still standing there. I awed.

It seemed like he knew I would come, that I would return back to fetch him. He knows that I'm in love with him so he wouldn't leave a chance to not let me fall deeper but this time I'll take the risk. I'll pick him up from the spot where he's been standing for two minutes now even if it means for me to feel more for him.

"You're back." He smiles getting in the car throwing his bag on the back seat as soon as he gets in.

"I hate regrets." I tell him honestly and start the car.

"I wanted to talk to you." He breaks the five minutes of uneven silence.

"About Madeline." He adds. I leave a small air from my nose showing him how important his topic seemed. He wanted to talk about her, his other girl.

"I don't know what to do. I'm just so confused with everything that's going around." He continues looking at me.

"If you want my suggestion, simply go date her. Ask her out and be happy." I don't want to mention me on this topic because I never was, was I? I was never in it.

"I weirdly trust you, a lot." Yeah, right. "I don't want to hurt you by my decisions." he sounds different. What he said sounds so true and honest but I can't let myself fall for it. He just wants attention, I believe. My uptight self takes over again.

"You actually think I like you, don't you? Well, guess what? I hate you and the only suggestion that you would get from me is that you should just go date her." I try to make him realize that I'm not hurt and won't be too. Whoever he dates won't change my mind or decisions about him.

"What is love according to you?" It seems like my definition of love is a big deal for him just for a while but I know it isn't.

"Love?" I turn to look at him once and look back on the road again. He nods, smiling slightly. As if he knew that it would only end up defining him, but I won't let him win this time. I won't let him feel good about my feelings for him.

"It's when beyond all their flaws and mistakes, you see their perfections... You want to be there next to them, protect them and always want to see them happy no matter how much it costs... You want to share everything with them, happiness and sadness. And it's absolutely not looking for someone with a great future, but is to make them your amazing present. When you find yourself in a situation as such? That's love." I end up looking at him again and I see him staring, glaring I guess.

He's probably thinking that I'm naive and stupid to believe and have faith in such petty thing.

I raise my eyebrows to see a reaction from him, but he stays quiet. Right when I turn back to look at the road again, he speaks up, "That was... Beautiful." His words take me by surprise.

I didn't expect him to agree with it because he doesn't understand the meaning and how we feel when we actually are in love. So his response just throws me off for a little longer than it should have.

"So.. You're telling me that you are still confused if you should date Madeleine or not after about ten months? You should ask her out. Go on a date or something at least once and try to understand her better. "I tell him with a very thick voice. It almost feels like I have an Adam's apple. It feels so heavy that I stop my breath for a few seconds and take a huge gulp.

"We went out already." His words take me by surprise again for the hundredth time since I first met him. Almost everything he says every time is just unbelievable and surprising to me.

"So?" I raise my eyebrows still not looking at him.

"I want to get your opinion on this."

"You should probably date Madeline anyways. She really likes you and it's already too obvious." I lie; she doesn't like him as much as... any other girl would.

Even though mentioning Madeline's name makes me feel horrible, I just don't seem to get a hold of myself if he stays here with me talking about his life and decisions on it. It will just make me feel like I matter to him, like he cares about me, whereas the fact is that he doesn't and everyone knows.

While I wait for him to say something, but he doesn't and it just gets me annoyed. This silence between us makes me suffocate, him and his lies and all those other shit he carries falsely around me doesn't let me breath. I know that he lies, always does indirectly or directly, but it eventually just ends up leaving me hurt and shattered. So this time again, I won't let him win.

"You know, you should leave. Right now." I pull over my car in the middle of the road, stretch my arms to grab his bag from the back seat and I hand it to him, "Here."

He stares at me with his innocent but at the same time disappointed look. I feel bad for treating him this way, but this is how it should have started with from the beginning itself. I should have pushed him away from me and my sight way before today. I feel bad; hurt seeing him turn his back from me, but it's for the good. I know it is. He'll be extremely happy, Madeline loves him and I won't be around him to bother anymore so this is it. This will probably be the last time I'll be found smiling or crying for him. My tears slowly crawl down my cheek while I start the car and it doesn't seem to want to stop at all. It keeps on falling and I can't hold back my own tears.

I've always been really bad at goodbyes. Not with my dad, not with my sister and this time not with Dylan too.

"Aren't you going to the Halloween dance this year?" Mom asks during breakfast, I never do breakfasts but for the last few days I am. I finish my orange juice and try to act like I didn't hear her, but she keeps on staring at me.

"You aren't good at it." She comments on my childish behavior.

"I'm not, happy?" I rudely answer her before leaving and she doesn't say anything. Usually Grace interrupts the silence and takes away the attention from me, but this time she's not here to do that which makes me miss her awfully.

While I try to find my car keys for five minutes in my bag, I just can't seem to find it anywhere. It's been such a bad morning already. I walk to home wanting to get away from mom's millions of other questions; I hear her talking on the phone with dad.

"No you won't see her. How many times -"

"-Okay, I get it, but this is not the right time."

"-she just left to school."

"-no please don't create any scene there. She is already getting very low grades."

"-how the hell do want me to face her after that? She's been thinking-"

"-For god damn sake!-"

She doesn't move an inch the whole time while she is on the phone and after dad hung up on her, she stands up and almost trips but she grabs a hold of the top of the chair.

I see her calling up dad again six times in a row, but it seems like he didn't pick up. I plan to leave taking a cab until I hear her sob. I turn around only to see her on the floor crying. She didn't even notice the main door slightly open and she starts crying. She usually notices the tiniest thing around her. The next second I look back at home, the door is shut.

She was telling dad to not come to my school and to not tell me something but I want to know what she wants to hide from me.

What would she hide from me?

I get in the cab and reach school earlier than planned when I hear that my dad is calling me during lunch it doesn't really surprise me. Why is dad coming when mom told him not to? That's the only thing that I want him to answer right now. What's more important to him than to listen to his wife? Ex-wife..

But mom has always been the mean one. She's probably trying to make dad stay away from me even though if he wants to be with me. She just doesn't like people getting too close without her knowing she's always been that selfish. That is why she has an affair with one of my dad's colleague. She is just a greedy and self-obsessed women nothing else.

I hate her and Dylan. Actually, I don't even know whom to hate. We hate those, whom we claim to have our right to hate on, don't we? But Dylan's not mine and neither does mom act like I'm her daughter.

I just don't know why I'm always left confused and alone.

Walking to my dad after five years, I can't even smile because I feel like I'm going to hell. Walking towards this man who left me in the midst of the time and didn't consider me his daughter, it's killed me hundredths of time already. This feeling of being pushed away is getting too overwhelming.

"Hey, dad." I fake smile.

He turns around to look at me and hugs me kissing on my forehead as I see him smiling. I couldn't be any happier than this that he missed me too.

"I'm here to tell you something about your mom. I want to make things clear." He slowly slides his hands into his pants.

"Yea, go ahead." I smile at him for the longest time now. I don't care what he talks about; I just want to be here with him, breathing the same air after all these years.

"Your mom... what you know about her is half the truth." He sadly starts.

Did she have more affairs? Did she do something more badly? What happened? I want to ask him so many questions but he words don't seem to come out and dad continues.

"I've... I've made mistakes too. Long before she did." I raise my head now, in disbelief and utter confusion.

What does he mean? He...? No.

"I couldn't love her the way I should have. I was in love with someone else when you weren't even born. I was married to your mom but I had other things going on which is why while she was giving birth to you, I wasn't there for her. I wasn't there for six months after you were born. I used to be a drunkard-"

"-dad, that's enough." I don't want to hear any of these.

"You made me hate her all these years! I've been treating her like a stranger for five years and now you come back saying that she wasn't at fault? How could you? How could you make a daughter despise her mother so much?!" My eyes are bloodshot and I didn't realize I was screaming this time.

"I'm sorry, Stell. It came out this way but I was ashamed and your mother didn't want me to say anything to you." He tries to grab my arms trying to hug me but I reject his arms from locking to mines.

"You.. can leave now." I stammer.

"Honey.." He whispers, his voice as thick as mine implying that he's in tears too. I quietly wave my hand to him signaling him to stop, I stare at my feet for the longest minutes and he leaves, just like that.

"Stella." I hear a voice from behind walking closer to me and as soon as I turn around I hug this person.

We stay quiet for ten more minutes only the sound of my voice echoing around the room. I've never felt this comfortable in anyone else's arm and when I'm finally done sobbing I plan on knowing who this person this. I surrender myself because my emotions are too heightened and I can't think.

As I step back and face upwards to look at this person, like always surprising me by his presence its Dylan again.

Dylan Edward Darrington, Even though it sounds weird and strange, I'm in love with both his name and him

CHAPTER 11

Unaware of the bliss

"If something ever happens, don't remember me as this girl. Remember me as someone better." I don't know what I'm saying, but I just feel like I won't be seeing him from today onwards after what happened yesterday and today.

"I'm sorry.. What? Why are you talking like something's going to happen to you?" His puzzled face gives a hint. He is really stupid.

"No... Nothing. After what you just saw.. I don't know what's going to come next." I stare down at my sneakers and his.

"Sorry, but I didn't see anything and that person.. Is he a teacher or something?" I look back at him again and again, his face looks the same, puzzled.

I sigh. He didn't see anything but the worst part is I was hugging him that too for a few minutes and this move I made towards him, makes me go crazy.

"No, he's not and I'm sorry." I speak uneasily and I actually am inside too. I literally hugged him, but it was because I lost control over my feelings, emotions and myself.

"I.. didn't mean to-" I add while he speaks instead.

"-You didn't mean to hug me?" I look up at him in a shock for he just said that. My eyes widened and for a while I feel amazing, this atmosphere between us at the moment. It feels like he knows me so well and like he can actually read my minds.

I nod and smile at him as he smiles along.

"I was just passing by searching for Dave, did you see him?" He tries to change the topic and it works.

"Um.. Dave?" I look around.

"Actually, never mind. You should better go wash your face first; your makeup is all smeared up." His lips making a thin line right after.

"What? It is?" I raise my eyebrows and cover my eyes in shame.

"I mean... it's not bad? But.. you can go wash up or something. I hope you feel better." He pats on my left arm and he slowly turns around to search for Dave.

"Shit!" I almost yell once I enter the washroom and look at myself in the mirror. I didn't put much make up except for some eyeliner and mascara. It's all over my red and swollen eyes.

Dylan saw me like this; it's absolutely and unimaginably insane of me to look like this.

"What's going on with you and Dylan?" Chloe winks at me once we take our seats.

"I planned on moving on, again." my voice trails off in the last word, making this squeaky sound like a crappy mouse and I hate it because I can see Nathan staring at me from the corner of his eyes which is absolutely driving me nuts right now.

He should ask Melanie out, the girl he has a crush on during the parties not me or anyone who is in love with some egoistic guy.

Thinking about Nathan, I wonder how things are going between Dylan and Madeline. Are they still talking? They hung out, Dylan actually likes her and he is just trying to fool me like always.

I hate him.

"Care to share?" Sydney smiles at me, more like an evil smile thinking that I'm crazy getting all heated up for nothing.

"No, it's nothing." I smile back at her.

I was crying like a lost puppy today and Dylan saw it, my day couldn't get any worse.

"Hey, sup?" Sydney sits on the seat right next to me where Nathan should be but he isn't today. He is sitting with one of his best friends and I'm glad he is. I can't face him anymore.

"Nothing, really." I sigh, taking out my pencil case and textbooks from my bag.

"What's going on here? You've literally pushed me away for two weeks now. Will you please explain me all this shit?" she waves her hand as everyone's face towards us in amusement.

"Sydney, don't create a scene here. I don't want to talk about it right now." I try to make her understand that I don't want any drama, but she being her very self leaves the class making it obvious that she is mad at me. As I look around I see everyone still looking at me and I raise my eyebrows to them, which makes them feel uncomfortable, everyone turns back to the board again.

I'm so tired of trying to explain people that I'm not ready to give them any reason.

"What just happened to Sydney?" Chloe asks me with her eyebrows more close, making it look like she's never seen Sydney outburst this way.

We all have seen Sydney overreacting over petty issues, she holds grudges and it's better to ignore than to explain and try to make her understand because she just won't.

"She was asking me stuffs that I'm not yet ready to talk about." I open my text book and start scribbling over the last page of it and Chloe turns back at her table to do her stuff.

Right after ten minutes the teacher enters the classroom, smiling brightly as usual.

I see mom arranging the dinner table for us and I just stare at her for few minutes standing still like a dumb person who's been hating her mom for ages now. She always tried to act like everything's fine, she always smiled but today morning right after I left, that day right after dad left, five years back too, she's been crying the whole time without letting me know. She's tried her best to hide it from me but I know that she is somewhere just like me, hurting, crying and hoping for things to change but not everything can be rectified, can they?

We just hope a little too much than we should and I see where my story is going, I'll end up exactly like how mom has right now. I'll be alone, shattered and unbearably hurt like her just the way she predicted. I remember her words now, that day when she came into my room to talk about her and dad. She said she was in love with dad, but things changed and it hurt, but we can do nothing to stop the mourning.

Her words surround me by all the insecurities I could've never imagined of feeling and it feels horrible, like this is never going to stop. This suffocation of finding out about all the unravelling truths about life will just bury me in here and I won't be able to do anything but see him leave. He's going to leave just like dad did. I'll try my best to act like nothing happened, but it will happen, it's going to hurt and the worse thing possible, I'll lose all my faith in these words called 'Love' and 'Care' that I believe on the most right now. I know I'm going to lose them sooner or later, but like always I choose to get hurt, again.

Just like mom.

"Honey, what're you doing right there and where were you this late? Anyways, never mind, go take a shower and let's have dinner." She goes back to the kitchen again, makes some noise of plates and returns back with a couple of plates and glasses.

As soon as she places them on the table, she looks at me again, worried this time.

"Did... did something happen at school?" She walks closer wiping her hand with the teddy bear apron she's been hanging around her neck. It's her favourite apron.

"No, I'll be right back." I'm her daughter anyways. I tend to hide my feelings just like her. I turn around and climb the stairs to my room.

While I'm taking a shower, I can't help but think about how mom and dad fought, how I broke up with Evan, how I hate Dylan, how Grace left home, how I hid my feelings from Daisy, how I treated Sydney today, how I didn't care about the innocent Nathan, how Emma's friendship is falling apart from Madeline, everything is going wrong and I can't do anything about it.

Everything.

Half of this hell- like feeling started after I met Dylan, it's all my fault and I don't know why I tend to always lose my control over my feelings towards him.

I just can't stop this feeling, I already think it's too late to try and hide it because I know that Dylan thinks I like him and he is nowhere wrong.

I don't want to like him, but he makes me feel like.. I have to.

As I close my eyes when rubbing shampoo over my hair, I remember seeing him for the first time at the locker, party, road, hallways, class, April fools.

How he played a prank and made me feel like he actually cared.

This mixed feeling I have for him, this hatred and admiration both only makes me think of him more and time and again, this only reminds me of how foolish I have been, thinking that he actually might have had any feelings for me. I might have gone completely insane to think that we would have any mutual feelings.

We've never had anything in common and won't have in future too.

I try to finish bathing fast after thinking about all the happenings around for a long time and I hear mom calling out my name, yelling which I've always hated.

I smile in the water while washing off the soap and shampoo, I'm starting to like her yell at me. Why can she be so impatient all the time? I ask myself as I laugh within myself and deep down I can feel that something might go right from now on.

I can make things go right.

I pull my white shorts to my waist and put on my black tank top right when I'm dry and out from the shower.

"Spaghetti?" I uncover the lid of the bowl and put some on my plate. Her plate is already full and she smiles weirdly at me.

"What?" I raise my eyebrows, taking some pasta on my fork and rotating them.

"You look cheerful today, I haven't seen you this way for a long time." she takes a sip of water and smiles again.

"If you're going to ask me about Dylan, then let me tell you first myself. I'm moving on and I don't like anyone right now." I take my first spoon and take a sip of orange juice.

"Sounds legit." She pulls some pasta from her chopsticks, so annoying. She likes the form of Japanese eating style like how they eat their noodles with chopsticks and she sometimes even eats the raw fish, what they call it "Sasha".

"Ha?" I laugh at her remark.

"I just think you're right about moving on, It's a good thing." She takes a sip again.

"Can you stop it with your chopsticks, I hate it. The fetish you have for Japanese food." I tell her and try to make an annoyed face.

"Oh! Let's have sashimi tomorrow."

"What's that?" I raise my eyebrows.

"Salmon. It's called sashimi, but sushi is more common and easier for you to pronounce even though it isn't basically called that."

"Oh, Sasha? Hell no!"

"It's SUSHI for god sake. It's already been years correcting you. Sometimes you call it shisha, sometimes susha, sometimes sasha!?" I laugh at her for how much she hates me for calling it wrong.

"Okay, susha!" I widen my eyes and continue eating more of my pasta.

"It's *Sushi*." Her eyes even bigger than mine while she emphasizes the word.

"Okay, whatever. Don't want to eat that." I made it clear to her already ages back about me not liking her taste, but she keeps on forcing me to get into stuffs she is into.

Once I'm done with my Pasta I leave the dishes on the basin and walk back to my room crossing the hallways.

"I'm NOT going to have Sasha tomorrow." I remind her, just in case she changes her mind.

"**Sushi**." She says louder this time like I care about the name.

"It's Friday! TGIF! TGIF!" Chloe cries happily.

"What're you doing tonight?" Daisy asks me during lunch break ignoring Chloe.

"I think I'll go have dinner with mom. I don't want to have Sasha though."

"Sasha?" She folds her arms.

"It's a Japanese thing, what're you doing though?" I don't want to explain her about the things going on between mom and me.

"I'm planning to have a gathering too. You can join us whenever tonight at my place. It's going to be a whole lot of fun." She smirks.

"Sure." I smile and the bell rings for our class.

As soon as I enter I see Dylan sitting behind my usual seat. I'm having a good day so far and I'm not going to let him spoil it this time.

"Hey." he raises his eyebrows quickly as soon as I sit.

"Hey." I repeat.

"Are you going to Daisy's tonight?" He asks excitedly.

"I'm not quite sure about that." I answer him, honestly like every time. I hate it how I'm so honest with him. I could've just said an accurate answer like yes or no but I don't know why I don't.

"Oh, cool. So what happened yesterday? I mean.. well only if I'm allowed to ask?" He coughs.

"It's none of your business, but I don't want you to think that I like you or some sort." I change the topic; I was dying to talk about it and clear things out with him.

"You.. Don't?" he almost whispers and leans forward.

"I don't want to." I tell him. I turn around to face him and add, "Go ahead, laugh at the girl who loved too easily."

We are having like an extra class where they teach us how to maintain good habits and manners within and out of school life. They teach us how to exercise and all too but we have a schedule for every lesson. Today we will be playing some games.

"No... I don't intend to." He whispers again.

"I sometimes quite don't get what you want as in what your intentions are to always make me realize how strong I feel for you." I'm louder this time, but hopefully the class is too noisy for anyone to hear what I just said.

"Don't accuse me." He sounds annoyed.

"I'm not and I'm extremely sorry for I made you feel that way. You must be really busy right now, I'll try to keep my distance and I'm sorry again."

I'm sorry for I fell in love with you, douche bag.

As I look around again, scanning if anyone heard me which they shouldn't, I see Isaac and Carter staring at us.

Isaac is one my closest friend and Carter is one of Dylan's best friends. Even though Dylan talks to Carter as a friend, but I know that somewhere Dylan is reminded of me by Carter every time they talk. I can notice by his uncomfortable answers and awkward smiles.

"You don't have to be sorry. Actually, I'm sorry for being a jerk. I know that I've made you feel ridiculous and it's my entire fault, for I made you feel this way." He sighs and looks sad, regretful somehow. I nod and turn back to my desk facing the board and to the teacher who is explaining about the rules. Her hands motioning around, lips opening and closing but I can hear nothing. I can't hear her at all but..

His words.

Lies, those were all lies. He chose Madeline over me which clearly means that he's been looking at her exactly the same way he does to me and that's how she felt for him.

He used the same trick, the glaring shit.

> *I have a very big crush on you but sadly I'm just a bug and you are a garden.*

This line strikes me hard which is absolutely true, I'm just a bug.

As the bell rings after half an hour of playing some shitty game, Dylan smiles at me and I smile back, forgetting about everything that just happened like every time.

This rushing feeling I have for him every time he smiles at me, I can't describe how good it feels. This uncontrollable infatuation and fondness of his presence that throws me back every time with my own move and words I use around him is just incomparably different and beautiful at the same time.

I don't know what's going to come next, but right now, he's my one infinite fidelity.

I've longed for these words to come out of my thoughts for months now and I can't stop thinking about how much I smile every single time his name is mentioned. I'm myself now, which feels like after ages, I'm actually happy this time. He's never done any harm to me, it's just my assumptions and hopes going to a different track, making me feel extremely sorry for myself but that's not how I want it to feel. I don't want to feel sorry towards myself. I never planned on falling for him.

I want to live out with what I need even though I know I want to hate him, but I need to let my feelings come out so that I find out what's going to happen without feeling like it's the part of my plan. I know it's not going to feel quite the same, but it's never going to change me.

This time it will be about me not Madeline or anyone else and just for some time, I want to be carefree and feel like I matter to myself.

"Bye" I pat on his back this time leaving him standing there all startled after how I changed from an outburst, uptight self to this patting person like him.

CHAPTER 12

Hi I am Stella

"Are you okay?" Mom asks me right after I came from Daisy's place.

"Yeah" I nod locking the main door from inside just in case, someone sees me in this state.

I saw Madeline on Dylan's lap, how am I supposed to act like? I just left the place and hurried home only to see the last person I wanted to talk to, mom but my tears crawl over my cheeks to my lips, leaving the sorrowful sensation that has been hiding behind my tears. I really hate him.

"I lied, I'm not okay." I turn to mom and hug her tightly, wanting to never see her leave like everyone.

"I thought you gave up on him already." She understands me so well.

"I'm close to giving up." More tears, more lies. I don't know when everything's going to fall in pieces but it should really soon or I'm going to lose the little space I have inside for trusting someone I love.

"This should not be happening again to you, don't you get it?" She rubs my back.

"Mom, will you just support me in this? Please? I insist." I want her to caress me not say things against my feelings for Dylan.

"I just can't believe this? Don't you see the border line already? Everything is happening exactly the way it did 20 years back! I don't want to see you falling just like me, honey. I don't!" Mom pushes back, looking around with rage and power on her face. I've never seen her this way, what's so wrong about loving someone?

"I can't help it, mom. I love him." I'm now trying to make her understand about my feelings and I didn't realize that I've stopped crying.

"I did too." She lowers her head trying to hide her face and emotions.

"I know what you went through and I was extremely surprised to know about it for this thing should've never happened to a beautiful woman like you." She is beautiful; she would've found a better person than my dad. She is nice, strong, beautiful and smart, she deserves better.

"That's exactly why I'm scared. You're like me and he is just like your dad. He isn't sure about anything at all. Just look at how long you had to wait for him?" She is comparing my love life to hers now; she thinks that I'm going to end up just like her. Alone and hopeless.

"I didn't wait at all. That's what is different between me and you. You waited, but I turned my back and every time I wanted to walk back on my track again, I see him there which makes me want to be there for him to help him go somewhere." I don't know what I said but the next second my words are out, I'm regretting it already like every time.

"Go to your bed." She doesn't look at me, she's already had too much and I totally understand why.

MONDAY...

"What's going on? Why am I forgetting things?" It's been few days now, I've been forgetting every little thing like leaving my car keys every single day, forgetting to close the door, turning off the air con, my bag many times, way to home, my car colour while in the car park I couldn't recognize my car one day.

Just now I forgot to take my backpack, I left it on the breakfast table itself. I've never been this clumsy and unorganized.

"This might sound absolutely insane but you are turning into a supernatural being." Mom puts down the jar of water on the small table next to the window.

"I'm turning? Turning to what?" I move towards her because I've always sensed something different in this city.

"You don't have to be scared. It's just a little part of your memory that will be gone." She looks down to her toes.

"What do you mean by gone?" I don't blink at all; I don't want to miss a single move of hers.

"Forever" She still doesn't look at me.

"No Mom, I've recently just felt amazing about everything around me! What am I going to forget?" I don't want to forget anything. I panic thinking of the things I might forget.

"Your best and your worst memory. Things around you should balance so that you won't create any triumph while turning. Memories that can hold you back, they will all be erased for good." She looks at me now like she has lost a huge part of her best and worst as well. She probably did.

"Will I forget about you and dad breaking up? Because that's probably the worst I can remember." I ask her with a shaky voice. I haven't ever asked her anything about dad.

"Yeah, I think you certainly will." She thinks I will... She slowly lifts the jar again, nervously this time.

"What am I turning to? Because I know I've always sensed very weird stuff in this town. Is it vampires? Werewolves?" I curiously ask her.

"A wizard." She answers me with something I didn't expect her to.

"A witch?" I snap.

"No, they are two different beings. Wizards are the good ones. I'll explain everything to you when the time comes. Now, you just need to attend your classes and act normal." She suggests, still holding the jar uncomfortably.

"How can I act normal? A wizard? Is not a small thing. I need to learn things about it and the impacts." I ignore her nervousness and still try to investigate.

"You actually believe me." She looks surprised now.

"Were you lying?" I raise my eyebrows hoping what I just asked to not be true. Hoping she wasn't lying.

"No, honey but when my mom first told me about this I couldn't believe her for a few days." I sigh a heavy one.

"Show me what you can do." I ask her and I take the jar away from her hand because it's been distracting me.

"Don't be scared, but I've always wanted to teach you." She hurries and takes a deep breathe.

She lifts her hands in the air and motions it to the dining table and the table breaks apart in a second. My eyes widen as I couldn't believe what I just witnessed with my bare eyes. She breathes out, her voice sounding very audible.

"We don't break things, we put them back together." She looks at me and smiles. As I turn to look at the broken pieces, the table is back to its six year old position again. Not broken at all, no scars and no sign of it ever being broken.

I smile at her joyfully. I want to be a wizard, always wanted to be something I'm not. t. I feel like my heart is ready to burst.

As I enter my class for the fifth day after I found out about me being a wizard, I gracefully walk to my seat with the *'I can control you'* look.

Mom told me that she had to make a report on my fake accident. Just in case I forget a big part of my life, a car accident would be my excuse for that. All of my friends actually believe that though, how stupid of them. They seem to be very cautious around me these days and it's way too obvious already. Even if I had an accident for real, I would notice that by now.

It's Friday today and I'm going out with my friends for some drinks. It's going to be mad fun because everyone will be drunk and I can do magic publicly this time, they'll think that they're hallucinating.

Mom warned me to not attempt any magic in public, but I really want to try it. I've been reading books of magic secretly after school every day and the world of magic seems way more fascinating and interesting than I thought because I can actually do some myself.

As I grab my seat, everyone around me smiles because they believe that I've had an accident. Right when the bell rings for the extra class we are in, which happens once a week, the door slams.

"You're late." The teacher smiles at some students and within few minutes they enter with late slips.

While I'm texting Chloe under my desk, someone drops his or her pen near my feet.

"Can you pass me the pen, please?" he asks from behind.

"Sure." I bend down, hand him his black pen and smile at him brightly because he was one of the late comers today. I just love making fun of people.

"Stella, can I sit next to you?" Nathan rushes.

"Sure." The second time. I'm being really nice to people today.

I almost laugh at the gray-brown eyed guy behind me who is staring at me now. Nathan seems to be close to that guy somehow, they've been late together for the last 2 days. And as far as I know Nathan, he is a very nice guy like I've always thought he was. Even though he following me around completely drags the compliment to the floor, let's just take that as an exception. He is extremely nice in overall.

"You know Nathan?" the guys ask me surprisingly as soon as Nathan leaves for the washroom.

"Yeah. Why, shouldn't I?" I answer him with a question.

"No, I didn't mean that way." he hesitates his own words. He doesn't make any eye contact with me and I find it very weird for him to do that.

Right when the bell rings after our boring extra class, I walk out with Chloe, Sydney, Emma and Daisy. They act very protective towards me the entire time from class to the hallways which is very awkward and new at the same for me but I'm adjusting to these tiny changes of life.

I'm a wizard, I really want to scream boasting about it but I can't. I want to tell this to at least one of my friends, but that would only make things worse. So, technically my mouth is sealed and so are my hands. I neither can do any magic nor talk about it unless it's with mom. This is ridiculous.

"Do you know where dad is?" Mom calls me after school.

"Why?" I walk down the stairs to meet my friends downstairs. I told them that I could come myself. They wouldn't leave me alone for even a second.

"He isn't home yet." Mom sounds worried.

What the hell?

"Mom, I remember everything about you and dad. Stop pretending now, it's starting to annoy me every time you ask me about stuffs about dad and Grace." I get mad at her for pushing this *'you are going to forget your worst and best'* too much.

It's going over the line now; she's been calling me almost every single day investigating for what I might have forgotten.

"What did you forget then? It's starting to get me worried." I hear sounds of dishes in the background, she's probably doing dishes.

"How am I supposed to know what I forgot when I already did? Now please, I'm going to be late tonight so don't stay up for me to come." I hang up on her right when I see my friends walking towards me.

At nine, after we spent seven hours at the mall watching movies and playing random games at the kids section we go to the bar as planned.

Once we enter the bar we see a lot of our school students and my girls here who are making an entry to these groups of juniors and seniors, everyone is extremely excited and crazy to get drunk including myself.

I haven't been drinking or going out for a while so I think I need to and I want to do some magic here.

After everyone has a glass of something to drink in their hand, I plan to explore a little.

I see Dave with his friends waving at me and I walk towards them.

"This is Elijah, Elijah she is Stella." We laugh at the way Dave called his name. It's not supposed to be that way. I smile at Elijah, I know him.

"I know her, dude." He punches Dave and Dave starts giggling like a little baby.

"Okay, this is Isaac, which you already know. Oh! That's Carter the one who just left to probably get a drink."

Isaac pats on an empty seat next to him, "Sit." and I walk towards him when I see that gray-brown eyed guy again.

He notices me staring at him. He shrugs and stands up, "Hey, I'm Dylan."

"Hi, I'm Stella." I smile at him and we both sit after introducing ourselves and I see Isaac mysteriously staring at me.

"Sup?" I raise my eyebrows.

"No, nothing." He looks away. What just happened?

After 5 minutes I get a call from Ethan.

"Hey." I sigh. It's been really long since we last talked. I don't remember why we stopped talking.

"Stella, how's life?" he sounds different, did something happen? He sounds so sad.

"It's the same, what about yours?" I ask him and I walk away from the group of boys who are all drinking too much right now, pretty tipsy everyone.

"You've been dodging my calls for almost a year now." Scratch the sad part, he actually sounds terrible.

"I'm so sorry, I don't know why I've been acting like I'm all worked up but I didn't intend to turn things this way. I didn't mean to hurt you, Ethan." I walk past the door and lean against the wall where there's no one around but only cars parked at the front.

"Thanks for that. I know how annoying you get at times." He chuckles on the other side of the line and I smile here sitting like a retard, outside the bar apologizing to my ex for how screwed up I am.

"I'm really sorry." I sit on the stairs and start plucking out some grass from the floor that's been growing between the wooden floors which is matching the green marbles placed around the flower pots.

"So are you seeing someone?" He asks calmly as if my answer won't bother him if it was a yes but it's not so it shouldn't.

"I'm not seeing anyone." I sprinkle the grass around my converse and I start playing with it a little more by plucking out more.

"I haven't lost all my feelings for you." He almost whispers as if it's been a secret the whole time.

"I'm always going to love you, Ethan." I tell him as I try to make the grass move around with my hand without lifting them by touching and it works. Ten pieces of grass slowly move around my converse.

I am a wizard, I couldn't be any happier than I am now.

"Me too, Stella." Ethan says from the other end of the line and it makes me smile while he is saying these wonderful things I am able to do things he can't.

"Hey, that's cool." I hear a voice from behind making me panic and all the grass fall back to my shoes.

"I'll call you later." I end the line with Ethan in a rush and as soon as I turn back to look at the person standing behind me, tilting his head against the door making a thin line with his lips shaping a smile.

Shit.

Those grey eyes are bloodshot, he's drunk. I sigh and look back on the grass, they are flying by themselves.

"And you are..?" I forgot his name.

"Dylan Edward... Darrington, the dummy" He sounds so darn sick and he slowly walks toward me.

"Hi Dylan, I am Stella." I smile at him.

"Ms. Stella Hamilton, why are you always mad at me? Oops, sorry, you had an accident, but do you remember me?" His mouth smells like a bucket full of liquor. He is way too drunk.

"Yeah, I remember you. You are Dylan, who sits behind me in the class."

"No!" He walks closer and sits next to me, but I try to move him away from me. He looks at me in the eyes like he knows me so well.

"What?" I push his forehead away with my finger.

"You like me." He leans forward, placing his head on my shoulder and I cover my mouth because of the very unpleasant odor coming from his mouth and body.

Where the hell is Dave? I look around for Dave or any of his friends but I see none outside, everyone is inside.

"Are you seriously out of your mind?" I ask the drunken guy, but I know he's not going to answer me anyways, so I check my phone and see Ethan's text, *"Go home early and take care of yourself."*

"Don't lie.. I know you like me sooooo much." This guy sounds completely insane and he is getting on my nerves I don't know why.

I try to use magic to move him away from me, but he grabs my arms.

"Stella Hamilton likes Dylan the stupid guy, haha!"

"Oh my god!"

"Did I just call myself? Stup-?"

"Oh my god! This is hilarious!"

"You stay put, Stella! you are very very comfortable."

"Haha you know..-"

"-you are like my blue ninja pillow."

He keeps on talking to himself.

What the hell is wrong with this guy?

CHAPTER 13

He never will

"You better stay away from me or else I'm-" I try to warn him, whereas my words, stop in between as he leans in closer to me this time, too close to my face and his eyes are beautiful if I haven't mentioned them before which I feel like I have more than a hundred times.

"Or else you, what? What can you do to me?" He challenges.

"I'll stab you right on your gorgeous, tempting little eyes, you drunkard." I haven't sworn on anyone for so long and this feeling of being able to say and do anything scares me a little within myself now making me look away from this obnoxious self-esteemed guy.

"Wow! I've never heard you swear at me and if it's not too weird to hear, I find it pretty fascinating for this to come from an extremely uptight and future drawn little young lady." He smirks at me following with a very unpleasant yet bubbly laugh.

"Aren't you supposed to be drunk?" I roll my eyes and check my phone again thinking about whether to reply Ethan or not.

"Yeah, I'm tipsy but well, I was pretending to be drunk earlier." He leaves my arm now, he's been holding it for a few minutes and surprisingly I didn't remember to throw a fist at him for making such a dorky move.

"You were pretending?" I switch off my phone screen and I look at him; my eyes all wide open along with my ears to hear what he said once again. He saw me doing magic?

"Yeah, why? Am I supposed to be not knowing something? I heard you saying I love you to your ex-boyfriend." He raises his eye brows, still smelling like shit through his mouth. I hate the smell of alcohol and coming to know that he didn't see anything reliefs me. I shake my head and go through my phone again, checking Instagram.

"You really don't remember me, Stella?" He asks after ten minutes of awkward silence and I shake my head again while liking some pictures of my friends who are inside posting them.

"Wait, what did you just say? I don't remember you?" I wrap my phone with both my palms and intensely stare at him.

"No offense for what happened to you, but you are acting like you don't know me at all." He stands up and looks around as if he just commit some crime.

"So you mean that I used to know you?" Did I actually forget him? I should only be forgetting my worst and my best, but this is very surprising that I forgot I know him.

Who is he? Who was he to me?

"Yeah, you used to know me" He exaggerates 'used'.

"That's interesting." I look up at him and he smiles an awkward smile.

"You know.. Sometimes things aren't the way we want them to be as?" I don't know why I asked that but I just don't know the reason why I don't remember him.

I play with the grass again, this time reminding myself to not let them fly. This guy isn't drunk yet and I can't let him witness anything that he shouldn't be seeing.

"I know.." He stares down at the grass I've been spreading around my converse for the past 15 minutes.

I should call my mom right away and tell her that the memory I don't have any more is of this tipsy guy standing next to the door reminding me about him. I brush off all the grass away from my converse and stretch a bit while standing. My legs are numb and I can't move but I don't want to stay here any longer.

"You better call me the second you cross that door of your house." His words sound so compelling.

"Do I know you by any chance? Oh, I used to know you." This time I exaggerate 'used' with a smile.

As soon as I grab the door handle to open the door, he moves fast towards me and turn me by my arms to face him with a very strong force as if trying to hurt me. His grip is so strong I feel like I can't move my hands at all.

"You better." His alcoholic breathe airing my ears and the gap between us so less making me shiver, warning my body organs to stay alert and my nerves almost feels like it's not working anymore.

How can someone's each and every senses be so heightened all of a sudden just like that? I ask myself.

I lift his hands from mine and walk past him, leaving him alone standing next to the door. I bid bye to all of my friends once I enter the bar again and I leave for home with tipsy Emma because it's time to investigate something by myself.

This night has been hectic and whereas I was planning to perform magic in front of the drunk mass, I couldn't. Whoever he is, to me, he will pay for it.

"How's your love life, Emma?" I plan to start the conversation first, don't want to delay a second this time. I start the car and I almost hit a red car, I'm still really horrible at parking.

"Apparently, I don't like anyone, so I would be extremely delighted if you don't ask anything about me right now because we are discussing about you." She winks at me and that obnoxious little cunning smile she gives, it's extraordinarily beautiful.

"I wanted to talk about Dylan.", I confess.

"Or perhaps I might have guessed a name of someone else but likewise knowing you for over a year now, you've never talked about anyone else but him. How stupid of me to think about someone else for you, aren't I?" Her smart mouth is annoying.

"Well, you precisely know me more than I do." I smile at her stretching the corner of my lip.

"I've been telling you Stella since the day you told me about him I've always suggested you that he shouldn't be admired this way. He is a drug, you once get into it and you can't get away. It's going to take time, a very long time to get over him so you should start it now." She seems much more realistic when she's drunk and I love her for how she always stands by me.

"Why do you want this? Me to forget him?" I ask her.

"He's done nothing but hurt you from day one and here you are so pitiful and desperately seeking for at least a drop of his attention he hasn't given for several months." She speaks up.

"I'm not desperate!" I feel the heat all over my body.

"Oh, that's what you say." she whines.

Emma's been here for two hours at my place, she planned to sleep over and she's told me everything about how my feelings towards Dylan were utterly insane and beyond imaginable.

"So you mean that I've always wanted to hate Dylan Edward Darrington but I could never accomplish it until this happened to me? Until I forgot every inch of fiber I had for him." I ask still staring down at my hands which are placed on top of my lap. I haven't moved for the past one hour and I've known so much about myself that I had no idea about.

"It was just an accident, but I believe it's not a coincidence, a fate I must say for you to never love him again. I might sound insane, but it's probably a sign to move on and have a wonderful life with Ethan." She grabs my hands and covers them with her.

"I can't, Emma. I feel so empty, I feel like I've lost a part of my life and I need to put it back together. I need to at least tell him how I felt about him, how miserable every moment was for me since I first met him. I want him to know how my life has changed from the day he became a part of it, a part of me which I've always wanted to lose but now when it's finally gone, I want him to hear me out. I want him to hear my part of the story, how he made me feel worse about myself for falling in love with him." I stand next to the window, staring at the stars that seem to look so pretty and vulnerable, but they are huge and lifeless, they'll live for long with many like them but in the end they all end up dying turning into millions of pieces.

Their life so worthless, yet worth while for us human stare up at them to look for our dead dear ones hoping that maybe one day they'll hear our cries and come help us with our nightmares and sorrows. But as far as I know, they are just as helpless as we humans. *We all live to only die one day.*

I wonder if they even exist or if life is all about illusions and hallucinations?

"It's not going to be that easy to tell him." I hear my mom's voice and I turn to look at the broken women I've seen her as for five long years, she now looks different. She looks more strong, bold, powerful, confident, sad and happy both but not broken anymore.

"What do you mean? And what.. What.. happened to Emma?" I run to Emma, she looks unconscious on my bed with her eyes closed and mouth open.

"She was drunk, she spit out everything you wanted to hear. So, I just gave her a Goodnight sleep. A hasty move for a newbie like you, but you'll get over it. You are a fast learner if you aren't aware of it yet." She walks in closer to me.

"You eavesdropped." I look into her eyes, fearlessly.

"Indeed, I must have." She's been very formal to me since the day she found out I was turning.

"What do you want?" I ask her, jumping on top my bed and tucking myself with the fur quilt my mom bought for me long back when I tore my other one when dad left home. I had a very bad temper.

"You didn't tell me that Dylan was your memory that you forgot about." My mom looks hurt. I should've called her the moment Dylan told me about forgetting him.

"Oh yeah, I was planning to call you but it went out of my mind because of Emma and I thought it would be better to tell you in the morning." I look at Emma and look back at mom.

"I see. So, is he your worst or..?" She steps closer to the bed and sits down at the left end of it.

"I don't know, mom. I don't remember anything about him. You told me that I would only lose some memories, but I don't remember Dylan at all, even now!" I almost shout for I remember nothing about this guy.

"That's not possible. Unless you first meeting he was your best-" She grabs my hands and I get annoyed by her touch. I've started to not like it when people hold my hand, I used to love them.

"-And falling in love, my worst." I almost whisper completing her sentence and I remove my hands from her.

"You should sleep now, take some rest. See you in the morning." She smiles bending closer towards me while I nod.

"Good night, sweetheart." She places a small kiss on my forehead and leaves the room after turning off the lights.

I don't know Dylan, what kind of person you are and why I fell in love with such a selfish person like you, but I'll make sure one thing this time that I won't ever repeat the same mistake again, I'm never going to love you again.

"Thank you for coming." He sits down after I do.

"You had something to say?" I ask, coldly.

"I shouldn't have said anything last night, I'm sorry." Dylan apologizes.

"It's okay, really." I assure him.

"You didn't call me last night. I was waiting for your call until dawn." He hesitate his words and I can clearly see how horrible he is at hiding himself.

"I'm sorry, I totally forgot about it." I apologize to him this time. We must play an apologizing game, where he needs to apologize for every single horrible day I've crossed through before I lost all the memory of him. I want to blame him for everything that has happened to me and my friends, but something stops me, pulls me back from splitting any words every time I open my mouth to say something. I am planning on to being very mean and awful to him by my bitter words for all I have gone through but I sure as hell don't want to hurt him or anyone if they were in his shoes.

"I'd like to have a Hazelnut Macchiato, please." I smile at the young waiter who looks about 3-4 years older than us, early 20's doing part time for his university I suppose.

"Nothing else, miss?" He notes down something on a small notebook placed in his right hand and I shake my head, he is a leftie.

"Americano and any kind of pizza with extra cheese in it that would be all." Dylan smiles at the man.

"So where were we?" He looks at me and his smile fades away pretty quickly.

"About last night." I remind him.

"Oh yeah, Stella, you probably don't remember, but I've made you feel horrible all these months and I can't help but apologize for what I could never give you. I really wish that you could forgive me even though it's unforgivable." He takes a sip of water from his glass, he looks nervous.

"I don't remember anything so don't act like I do." I don't want him to ask me for forgiveness because just like he said, it's unforgivable.

"Still, I can't walk around school seeing you every day and feel guilty for how I hurt you. Especially now that you've forgotten me, only me? I feel like I'm in a living hell every time I see your lost eyes. It's unbearable." He sighs a very terrific sigh right when the waiter comes back to place the coffee's on our table.

"Long story short, I don't know you at all but right now all I know is that I let you become my happiness and that's where I went awfully wrong. That's where everything went wrong, you weren't my happiness and that's it! I don't care about how bad you feel for me or for yourself. You brought it to yourself and I can do nothing about it." I look around if anyone noticed my outrageous behavior, but luckily everyone are so busy eating they didn't give a crap about what this stupid young teenagers are talking about.

"I know and I'm sorry for I wasn't your happiness. I'm sorry." He looks down not making any eye contact with me. I don't know why this guy acts like he cares so much about me, but he just seems like someone who has never lost. But this time he will. He will lose for what he's got and I'll make sure of it to be nothing.

"You don't have to be sorry." I don't know why I say this to him, but my words are against my will. I don't hurt people like him; I don't want to be someone who hurts the people that care for others more than themselves.

"The hardest things to let go are the things that you never really had, you've probably heard of this before." I add. I try to make him feel like I'm hurt inside, but I'm not, I don't feel anything.

"I know." He whispers and says nothing.

"I hope you enjoy your extra cheese pizza." I leave the table and him alone there. I don't know why I want him to feel like I hate him, but it's all I want right now. It's all I've got.

I don't get it; I can't see why I liked him so much that magic had to take my memories of him away from me.

"You are seeing that guy again." My mom says from behind right after I enter the wizard's house.

"I'm not seeing him; I just wanted to clear things out. I wanted to never fall for him again, which is why I-" I try explaining her but everything happens too quickly.

"So you think that hanging out with him was the best thing to do after all that's happened?" She sounds mad and it doesn't make any sense at all for the way she is asking me about it.

"Why are you so offended? I don't like him, okay?" I almost yell.

"Oh please, Stella! Don't play with me." She shuts the door behind me within a second and grab my arms.

"Mom, no-"

"You're seeing him again for god sake, stop lying!" What? I ask her within my breath. My eyes are wide open; I don't know why she is thinking that way?

"Mom" I call out her name to make her listen to me once.

"I know that deep down inside, you still love him. Your feelings are fighting with each other." She says loudly.

"No, mom!" My scream, my voice as audible as hers this time.

"Your feelings are fighting for him!" She raises her voice and I'm no less, I'm her daughter by any means.

"Enough!" I cry which makes all of the mom's ancient pot clatter along with her.

"I don't like Dylan!" I scream at the top of my voice, "I'm sick of hearing it from everyone, from Dylan himself was enough to hear already!" the windows bang as if a very strong storm is close by and that storm was me.

"Stella, breathe in and out. Look into my eye and try to find your anchor, focus." she steps towards me as I keep on staring at her eyes and I see nothing. It's empty, but this emptiness is familiar. It keeps me from ruining the house and the wind slowly calms down.

"What did you see?" mom asks me panicking around checking if any of her precious pots has been scratched by my rage or not.

"Nothing, it was empty. I couldn't think of anything." I inform her. She keeps on moving around still observing every single side of her million dollar pots.

"But the emptiness was not unfamiliar to me. I've had this feeling before but I don't know when." I tell her the fact and she stops moving around, keeping down the last pot without checking it.

"Your friend just woke up. Go check her, she might question for the loud noise and probably an earthquake." Mom doesn't face me, I know she is scared. I screamed like a mad man and she looks terrified, I'm a monster to make her feel that way.

"You're not." She whispers.

"You're not a monster, Stell." She looks up at me with her eyes full of tears.

"Mom, how could you-? You- you can read my mind?" I ask her as if I don't know the answer.

"Yes." She whispers again.

"No, it's just a delusion."

"Stella, we are all different. We all have something unique and this is what I am, I can read minds." She raised her eyebrows and I believe her.

"What's my special power, then?" I don't move an inch from my spot.

"I have no idea. It's been so many days since you turned but I don't know why you can do nothing but basics." She takes two steps towards the sofa.

"Why?" I ask her.

"You'll first have to erase Dylan from your mind, you should stop liking him. It's stopping you from knowing yourself." She looks at me as if I would agree on that.

"I don't like him, how many times do I need to remind you that?" She sure as hell doesn't understand English.

"Stop thinking about him then, I'll believe you and you won't need to remind me time and again once you do that." She says harshly.

"I really don't love him, mom. I remember nothing and I have no feelings for him." I remind her again and it's going to be my last time telling her.

"That's what you believe because everyone says so. You believe them and this is why you act like it. You still like him." She sits down on the sofa beside her.

"I.. I need to go check Emma if she has any questions about what happened earlier and she's probably sober right now." I tell her changing the topic about Dylan and I climb up the stairs going to my room.

As soon as I reach my room, I close the door. Emma's not on the bed, but I can hear water showering from the bathroom.

Mom was right. Somewhere deep down inside me, I still like that blue- grey eyed guy sitting behind me in class who made me see hell on Earth.

Emma comes out with a towel wrapped around her body and she notices my worrisome face by far.

"What happened?" She asks wiping her wet hair with another towel which is my favorite one.

"I think I still like Dylan." I take few steps until I don't know where. I always don't know what I'm doing, where I'm going, why I'm going and it's the reason I always fall. I fall too hard and it cuts too deep.

"What? But you don't know him." She doesn't remember anything about what she said last night while she was drunk.

"Today, I lost my anger over mom for some reason and mom told me to remember something, an anchor. I thought for a while and I could see nothing but emptiness, but it was very cold, dark and I felt lonely. That emptiness calmed my nerves or I would have harmed mom any time soon." I try explaining her even though I can't tell her about me being a wizard but she is smart, I somehow believe that she can understand.

"And what stopped you from doing that?" She stops rubbing the towel to her damp hair.

"That empty feeling I had, it's the same feeling I have when Dylan is around me or when every time I try to remember about the memories I had with him." I step closer to my bed and sit on the edge of it covering my face with both my palms.

"He is my anchor, Dylan Edward Darrington, who has turned my world upside down." My eyes are filled with tears, they are bloodshot and I lift my head to look at her. Show her how broken I am.

"How do you know all this?" She steps in closer.

"Last night he told me that I used to like him before my accident. I'm scared to even be around him, Emma." I pass her my dry cleaned pajamas, I placed earlier for her on the bed.

"Why is that? Why are you scared?" She starts putting on the blue silk I always lend her when she sleeps over.

"If I'm around him for even one minute, then..." I play with the fur quilt that my mom gave.

"Then?" She sits on the bed joining me to learn my awful side.

"I'm scared that I will fall in love with him, again." The tears in my eye don't want to fall in front of her and the lump on my neck gets heavier.

"And I'm more scared that he won't love me back." I look at her and add, "Again." The tears start crawling down over my cheek, reaching my lips and I wipe them off but the more I try to stop them, the more it falls.

"But- you said that he is your anchor." Emma hands me a tissue box from behind and the look she has on her face is so caring, I want to cry for that too. I don't deserve the caress. She's the second person witnessing my tears after mom and I hope she's the last.

"My first fear, it just came out to be true." Fear cuts deeper than the sword. I don't just love him, but I'm in love with him and losing my memories of him which are my worst, didn't change anything. And once again, Dylan won and I lost.

I hadn't realized how dark my life has become until I saw the little light after I forgot him. He doesn't love me, I'm sure I found that out a long time back, but I need to remind myself about that again and again from now on.

Despite every nerve in my body, wanting to tell him how wrong he is and how selfish he has been towards love I know the fact that *He doesn't love me and he never will*. I'll repeat it for my lifetime if I have to but I'll have to let the words resonate in my mind no matter what.

I'm done with hoping and as they say hope can always trick one in all sorts of insanely unrealistic scenarios, I fell for hope. A hope that maybe one day he'll feel the same way, but no that's never going to happen and I have to force myself into believing and accepting the fact.

He doesn't love me and he never will

CHAPTER 14

Standing apart

"So, how's Madeline?" I ask him.

"We aren't seeing each other anymore." He sounds serious.

"Oh, that was not something I expected you to say." I find myself feeling uncomfortable this time and I can't help but wear a fake smile. My old-self should be happy, she must be really happy right now but I'm not. I don't want to be the reason for people falling apart. If he likes her, he should date her as in a couple date not like us. Friends date.

"You want me to talk about you? I know that you've always wanted to remember how things were between us." He shows sympathy, but I don't need it right now, he does.

"Can we not talk about it, for a while?" I request.

"I'll consider that.." He jokes.

We laugh in unison, but right then Andrea makes an entrance, I haven't seen her for a long while. Since forever. I can't even remember she has changed a lot in just a few months.

"Hey, Dylan and.. Stella? Wow." She raises her eyebrows.

"I'll go grab a drink." Dylan rushes leaving us two ladies behind for our private moment, I suppose.

"Are you guys together, now?" She asks as soon as Dylan is out of sight.

"No! Absolutely not! We just bumped into each other outside school. End of the year, need to return all the borrowed books. I didn't return last semesters as well and even my friends so yeah, I brought them all today. What about you? Why are you here?" I explain to her, sounding more like excuses.

"Oh.. Well, I was here to meet someone and she didn't show up which means I need to drink by myself. Lonely, always been." She laughs and the last time I remember her is still not really clear in my head but I start remembering something.

Flashback:

"Don't look at him." Andrea says, bending close, to my ears.

"Why?" I turn to face her.

"Useless." She shakes her head like she's known him so well.

"You know him?" I want my doubts to be clear in just a second.

"Yeah, I know everyone. Actually, I know a heck lot of things about him." She boasts proudly.

"Oh, okay?" I raise my eyebrows.

"Where to begin with.. We started off being friends and we kind of went along well, but he asked me out one day. I couldn't help but laugh at it, deep inside." She laughs next to me and it feels horrible.

"Oh, okay?" I repeat myself yet again.

"I mean.. He's a nice guy, you can try and ask him out if you want to but it's not really worth it. Just saying, don't fall in love though." She laughs more.

"I won't, I don't even know him. I've only seen him for the second time?" I look at him now, he's talking to some guys and I know few of them. I've had classes with them.

"How do you know him?" She asks and stops laughing.

"Someone I know likes him, it's.. complicated." I answer her still looking at him and he doesn't even notice.

"His name is Dylan and he's from Washington, D.C." She gives me some of his information that I didn't ask for. Daisy never said anything about his name or where he's from and it keeps me thinking.

"Oh, I had no idea about his name." I smile at Andrea.

"Oh, okay then, I'm sorry I'll have to go check my friends." She leaves with a faint smile.

Flashback ends.

"You can join us if you want?" I smile.

"Nah, I'd prefer not to. I didn't think that you were serious last year when I first mentioned his name to you. That was quite a weird introduction I made of him." She is better now, more nice and simple.

"It was okay." I lie; it was not okay at all.

"Oh... just be careful. I need to leave now, don't want to ruin your romantic time with him." She winks hugging me before leaving. She is always leaving to go somewhere, always in a rush.

"It's nothing like that and see you." I hug her back.

"Say all you want, I do not believe you." She laughs and walks away.

"She left?" Dylan walks towards me from behind as if he didn't know. There's something bothering me the moment I see his face, he's pretending and he is very bad at it. I hate it so much that I'm the one getting to see it. I shouldn't know much about him, but he left me no choice. This was the last time we will ever be seeing each other.

"Yeah, she did and I think I will too." I smile at him and he returns the smile. He's tried his best to keep up with me in a very good level of interaction, but now that things are finally falling into pieces and I've finally seen the good in him that I always wanted to see, I can't be the very nice friend of Dylan anymore. Mom said he is human and humans are not trustworthy, humans love human and wizard love wizard. I can't break the rules that my ancestors made about not getting into a relationship with humans, but this is more than just that.

I had one million reasons to not fall in love with him, but now when I finally have the right and good reasons, they are meaningless. It's been two and a half month already since I turned into this wizard.

Talking about Dylan the devil, he has been very co-cooperative and understanding the whole time. We had good times and funny ones too, but in the end we both want the same thing, someone we want to love fully and neither of us can find that in one another. My friends think that we are almost in a relationship, but after all we have gone through for more than a year, we sure as hell are afraid to date each other. But because of our flirty jokes and endless talks we finally found a reason to laugh at together. We aren't arguing, hurting, acting insane or being hurt, but all these will surely come around one way or the other. It's just that the time we have had after all the shit we both went through, I'm glad I met him and I don't regret getting to know him as a good man. I'm not saying that I don't having feelings for him anymore, it just never stopped.

The only difference is that I used to like a bad person then and now this person is way better, loyal and honest. With time I figured that he is stupid, naive and goes completely insane at times because of the raging hormones but that's just how nature works and it would be hilarious if I say that I actually like it when he is himself because half the time I knew him was someone else, someone mean and cruel who would do anything to get attention.

"So, this is it?" I smile at him.

"Yup this, it is." He smiles back and looks around as if trying to recollect every memory of us in this place.

We came here many times and one night, it was hilarious. He got drunk and he would not stop speaking nonsense, I literally had to make him shut and I told him about how I shouldn't have liked him. He doesn't remember a single word as he was drunk but I hope that one day he will listen to a girl who is human, remember her words and will always love her no matter what the circumstance is.

She should be someone human, he wouldn't need to get done and over with. One who will always be there to protect him at his worst and make him laugh for all he has gone through his life. His hidden, secretive side should be familiar to her like how it was for me. Even though I didn't tell him anything about mine, which is far worse and more terrifying than his but he has a small heart, a very delicate one indeed that should be rubbed at times to ease his worries for petty issues which means the world to him. I would love to write poems about him, I thought. Poems about his sad life. Well, not poem specifically, they should be called lyrics or songs? I'm good with music.

I am remembering him pieces by pieces if I haven't mentioned that.

"See you around then." He breaks the silence.

After a harsh one year we are here, in the same old bar where our friends love to hang out at. We had our stranger eye contacts here, we drank here, he told me that I used to like him before the accident here, he made me remember him here, we've had our very good times here and yet after everything this is where it will be the end of us.

"Let's try our best to not see each other. Unless, we miss each other too much that we can't bear it at all." I joke and we laugh in unison. Him and I, we were never going to make it, but we are laughing at ourselves right now, we are laughing at our fate.

I sometimes wonder what you think about me, what I am to you. If, I mean as much to you as you do to me, but who am I kidding to again? Dylan and me, we are two completely bipolar. The feeling I had at first when catching him staring at me like a fool which made me feel like he liked me in the start and for which I fell for him, I wish it was true. I don't want to ask him because I'm scared it might be false, but hearing it from him that it was true would complete me, cure my scars.

"Bye." We say to each other and we walk away from the spot where we've been sitting and I've thought for almost one hour now. I know, we are like two psychopaths, but now his memories are good memories.

I'm going to miss his talk, his pointless topic that we have been discussing intensely about for hours, his laugh, the way he calls my name, the way it echoes at night and I'm definitely going to miss his voice.

We didn't date, just to make that clear. We were friends, more than that, but I would call us secret friends. No one knew about us hanging out or getting drunk every time after that, not even my best friends until last week and now we're done. Officially.

'New Year, New me' status's are all over social media, again. My New Year resolution would be... having fun every day. Bad joke, I still hate it every time I hear that and New Year's long gone. It's the middle of the year and well I wouldn't mind saying that I look like shit these days. Not talking to Dylan and not seeing him around was not hard but worse than that. I couldn't sleep for days, actually more. I feel sick, annoyed, I don't do my assignments and at the very least I feel lonely. Even though, Chloe and Emma had been there for me the whole time, Sydney's busy with her new one month boyfriend and I'm just not myself.

But this is for both of us, me and Dylan. So, I should try my best to work it out. He is happy, I can see that. He's moved on even though he didn't have any specific feelings, but from our friendship I suppose.

"You look awful." Chloe stands in front of me, observing my new self for the twentieth time.

"Thanks." I tie up my hair to a bun looking at the washroom mirror.

"You're going to tie your hair?" She raises her eyebrows.

"Yes-no! He likes it up, I better put it down." I untie it and look at myself in the mirror.

"You look better with your hair down." Emma smiles while stepping out of the washroom and washing her hand as she looks at me for now I look more than just awful.

Emma's been helping me a lot with getting over Dylan talk and it's better now than how it was yesterday.

"What do I look like to you? Honestly." I ask Emma.

"You look sad, but what if he figures?" She grabs her bag.

"He won't because... I will smile and he will believe it." I smile to myself in the mirror and it's different. It's fake.

"Out of all this chaos, the only person getting hurt of its outcome is you." Emma reminds me.

"I'm aware of that." I tell her taking few hair strands to the back of my ear. I tried my best to look fine today, patted some cream, crop top, white shorts, rings in my fingers, flower earrings and my white converse.

I didn't dress up bad to look like a broken hearted girl, Dylan won't even know anything.

"Stell." my sister calls me from behind after school. I haven't seen her for a while.

"Hey." I smile at her still the thought of her being over me to my parents strangling me to death, but I can take it, I've had worse.

"Shit, what happened?" her eyes widen as soon as we walk closer to each other and she notices my dead face.

"Nothing but how are you?" I pull her in closer to me for a hug.

"I'm good, what the hell happened to you though?" she sounds like mother actually she sounds like the older one among us, she hugs back.

"Nothing to worry about, I just couldn't sleep well for a few days." I tell her and she nods, trying to understand what my love life brought me to.

"Hey, you can tell me anything you want, okay? I heard about the accident." she says, she doesn't know anything about our family yet. I would love to disclose it to her, but let them surprise her.

"I know I forgot about Dylan, you don't need to hide the fact that you are desperately eager to know about how things are between me and him." I spit out those harsh words again. I don't know how she keeps up with me, but I love her for she tries her best to make me feel good about myself.

"I just wanted to ask if you talked to him. I would cry my eyes off if I knew that I forgot someone I love equally to my life." She says, how dramatic of her. I don't cry in public and he's nowhere valued equally to my life.

"I did." And as soon as the words come out I realize I don't talk to him anymore. We've chosen separate ways and it's for our own good, I can't be regretting it. Even though he told me that he's not seeing Madeline anymore, maybe another girl dropped into his life. He is a very dependent person, although we can't see it from the outside, but he is like a coconut, hard from the out and liquid inside. I bet he will have someone in his mind in a couple of months, though. He's scared of tiniest little things and even world's most stupid person can make a very good place in his heart.

"So did you cry?" my sister asks as we walk down the stairs.

"I don't know." I smile at her.

"I've never seen you cry, though." She looks sad, her voice not as exciting as it has been just a few minutes back. I never got to open up to her; I know she'll understand me once everything is done and when I'm ready to tell her.

"Okay.", I almost slip on the stairs, but I get the hold of myself the next second. I look at my sister when I walk normally again, admiring her for all she's got around her. Her life is perfect and I'm really happy for her. She doesn't have much to worry about, she never did.

"You look strong from the outside, but I know you're just as soft within, you cry, but you don't show." She looks at me with a smile. What she said was just the sentence I would use for Dylan.

"I don't."

"You're a bad liar; you should know that for a fact." She shakes her head, exactly like mom. She's so much like mom.

"Okay." My response is very short and I don't know how to make it longer because I have nothing to say.

"You sound really different and anyways I'll be leaving first. I'm taking the bus; you probably brought your car. See you tomorrow." She says, almost ready to jog.

"Yeah, see you around." I see her off.

As I'm waiting for Chloe outside school, I see Dylan. He's with his friends, I try to not look at him and I actually haven't seen him for days. I hope he doesn't notice my worked up face, I look all dumb.

It's unpredictable how he laughs aloud and passes by me as if nothing ever happened, like he doesn't have any idea of who I am. I should've seen it coming, it's Dylan. I can't keep my hopes high if it's about him.

"Stella." Chloe walks towards me.

"Thank goodness, you're here. Hurry, I can't stand seeing Dylan laughing around with someone and looking at me, show off." I roll my eyes and she laughs.

"Oh, okay." She says once she figures that I'm not joking.

"Why did I like him at first place again?" I ask myself as we walk fast to my car.

"You should have the answer for that." Chloe smiles while opening the passenger door and she gets in throwing her bag towards the back seat like how Dylan did a long time ago.

I remember him getting in and this was the exact same thing he did. I get in the black car and smile at Chloe; had I ever smiled at Dylan the same way?

"Apparently I was in an awful state of memory loss." I try to joke which is actually the truth.

"But there's something about the way he always made you feel with his words and presence itself, you told me that once. Everyone's noticed that." She winks giving me signal to start the car.

"I don't remember." I sigh, it's the only thing I know and will repeat since I don't know how many more days, weeks, months, years or probably for my entire life.

"He's a nice guy, you convinced me on that, but I'm not saying that I don't hate him." she looks at me as if she knows everything about me, as if she's my other half and I know that she is without any doubt. Emma and Chloe have been always there for me through thick and thin.

"I did?" I laugh.

"Yeah, you did." We laugh in unison because I don't remember anything. I miss Emma but she is sick today so she couldn't come to school.

After we take showers and are all set up to find a good romantic movie to watch on Netflix. Did I mention that my mom is an interior designer? Well, she is and she has a wedding to attend in Dallas which means she won't be home for tonight.

My phone vibrates and the ringtone I've had for six months is starting to annoy me. Emma tells me to take the call and that she would go make some popcorn and does.

I look at my phone screen, Dylan's call.

I think for a while if I should take it or not. For approximately 4 seconds of the first few rings, I remember everything that Emma told me about how I suffered to not like him, but after that the only thing that keeps me from ignoring in just one second is him. He is innocent and what happened was all my fault. I was the one who fell in love with him, I was the one who went to him talking about dating Madeline, and I was the one who led me to this. Emma was right and I know that all these that she told me are true, I can somehow feel it.

I have done horrible things in my life; one of the worst was falling for him.

I shouldn't be punishing him for what I did, "Hello?" I finally answer fighting myself to not speak any more word.

"Hey, umm... it was very stupid of me to think that I shouldn't talk to you. I can't not talk." his voice just the same as I hear inside me while trying to recognize if it's really him or not.

He adds, "I'm sorry." I was fine throughout the entire sentence until he said sorry. My heart falls hearing it, I don't know why. My body and their responses aren't listening to me these days and as I inhale and exhale some oxygen, it feels like my chest is a sack full of burdens and sorrows.

"Don't be." I almost whisper. I've missed him with every heart beat and I doubt if that's even less than reality. I couldn't stop thinking about him. I remember how a couple of weeks back we were walking side by side for 3 hours and it was the best feeling I've had in a long while. We didn't talk much, but we talked about him and how his personality changes when he is around strangers.

My old self must be very proud of me.

Emma plays a song from the kitchen and I can relate the lines like my own story, Ed Sheeran's 'All of the stars.'

I can hear your heart
On the radio beat
They're playing "Chasing Cars"
And I thought of us
Back to the time,
You were lying next to me
I looked across and fell in love
So I took your hand
Back through lamp-lit streets and knew
Everything led back to you
So can you see the stars
Over Amsterdam?
You're the song my heart is Beating

"That song" He giggles softly.

"Yeah, this song" I smile hoping that he would know I am.

"Actually, I'm going to New York for a week." He finally brings up to tell me, now?

"Oh." I don't know what to tell him, it's just a week anyways.

"When I'm back, I want you to forget about me. I want you to move on with your life and not look back even once. See you, then." He says so easily knowing nothing about how much it hurts even though I don't remember anything. It's unbearable and I hate it not only because I can't move on but more for it's about him I'm told to move on from. I swear if I could change anything in the world right now, I would change that very day I saw him next to the locker while Daisy was pointing him out for me to judge her crush. Pieces by the pieces I'll remember everything about him, but it really hurts like hell, I don't know why.

"Bye." I almost say, but I don't and he hangs up, I guess he heard me.

"Stella!" Emma shrieks as soon as I lift the MacBook. She comes running and hugs me right for 1 second and pulls back that very moment. She wasn't in the kitchen, she came from downstairs. She grabs my hands and squeezes it like it's a lemon and I laugh at her for she's been acting all insane.

"What.. what happened?" I finally ask her.

"Oh my god! Oh my god! Oh my god! Go downstairs and open the door, right now!" she says after taking a deep breath still laughing like a mad girl.

While I jog downstairs I miss Ethan, I wish Ethan was here to be with me in my worst. I haven't seen him for six years right before mom and dad broke up. I couldn't bring myself in front of him to tell him about my parents. I wish I did, he would be there for me unlike Dylan.

I open the door and to my surprise, I see the only person I want to see standing tall in front me with an absolutely beautiful bright smile, the man I promised to love forever and always. I smile back thinking that this must be my life's most perfect moment, my eyes fill up for one whole beautiful minute of my lifetime yet again without my permission tears of happiness crawl down my cheeks continuously.

We hug each other like we're some long lost couple which we probably are but we just aren't dating anymore. Ethan's in Texas, nothing in the world could make me any happier after my Dylan misery.

I lost my memory of the guy I was in love with who is leaving for New York soon and he has hurt me enough to leave any broken part. And well now here I am hugging my ex and crying in front of him, how predictable.

I'm definitely destined to become the world's most miserable person.

CHAPTER 15

Rejuvenation hurts

I've had this feeling before; I've hugged someone when I was extremely desperate for one. I remember myself crying on someone's shoulder. I don't know why I'm crying, but it looks like I'm at school. Why would I even cry at school? I was never bullied in Texas.

Sure, Dylan. I've hugged Dylan before, not sure when but I did feel relief after I don't know what tough time I had which literally doesn't matter right now.

"Holy shit, Stella. I've missed you so much." He kisses on my forehead as a greeting. His hands gently wiping my tears off my cheeks and all I can think of is Dylan doing it to me. Dylan wiping all my tears that I shed for him, it would be so worth it. I wish Dylan was here. I wish Dylan was like Ethan, sure about what he likes and what he loves truly.

"I've missed you more!" I scream and pull him by his wrists right after closing the door. He should definitely watch a movie with his former girlfriend I whisper to myself as I smile at my thoughts while dragging him upstairs to my room.

When we enter my room, Emma's wrapped up with a blanket and she is already watching the movie.

"You girls were watching a movie?" He asks looking at me.

"No, we planned to but she started without me." I roll my eyes.

"Oh, that's mean." he says aloud, but Emma doesn't move an inch from her spot.

"So how's it going with that guy?" he asks right after we sit on the sofa in the living room because of my dearest friend Emma whom I'll have to beat up right after I'm done talking to Ethan.

"Not that I have to tell you, but it's insanely terrifying and unimaginable depressing of how horrifying my appearance has changed into this devastated and outrageous shitty barrier -"

"- Stella! Calm your nerves for Christ sake. You're literally freaking me out right now. And damn those creepy words, why do you have so many in just one sentence?" He laughs and I do too.

"Sorry, I didn't realize that I was creeping you out." I apologize.

"So you were telling me?" He reminds me of what we were talking about, Dylan. We were talking Dylan.

"Um.. Basically, I'm a mess right now and I don't think I'll be the same girl again." I play with my fingernails and see a picture of smiling Dylan on my mind.

"Hey, I know I've lost the rights, but I think you should just move on from him." He places his hands on my shoulder and stands up trying to make me feel secure, trying to tell me that he's here with me and will be forever.

"Come here." He smiles at me for a hug and I hug him for a very long ten seconds. I needed it. I've gone through so much shit since Dylan and I last spoke. I feel like I would be dying if I didn't get this one hug. But somewhere around the corner of my heart and mind, I wanted Ethan to be Dylan. I wanted Dylan to be here and know everything about what he made me feel. I wanted him to tell me that it's going to be alright and he would never hurt me again, but even then I knew that Dylan would never do that. He would never know anything about this and I don't want him to either.

"So.. you want to talk about it?" He asks after five minutes, holding two cups of Black Tea on his hands as he walks towards me and the conversation goes on, hands one cup to me.

"Thanks." I smile, raising the cup of warm tea he made, not answering his question because I know that I want to talk about him but I know I shouldn't. The more I talk about him, the more I want him to be right next to me.

"Aw, not a problem." Ethan smiles and we sit back on the couch again.

"He's going to New York for a week." I finally speak up after finishing my tea and placing the cup on the table.

"So, what's the problem? It's just a week. He'll be back and you guys can sort things out." He places is cup on the table too and looks at me in the eye but I can't take it. I can't even look at his eyes. All I can think about is Dylan and how beautiful his eyes are.

"He said I should get over him until he returns. He said that the idea of us not talking at all isn't working. I think he means that we will be talking again soon but he does not want me to like him. He probably hates the idea of interacting with someone who has a one sided love towards him or maybe he just wants me to be around him all the time. Maybe he wants to see me get hurt; maybe he wants to hurt me more, maybe how much he has hurt me until now was not enough for him. Maybe he likes seeing me this way." And without realizing my eyes are full of tears, again.

"Just be positive, Stella. I know he's going to come around for your love." He tries to calm me down and I don't listen to him. I keep crying and my emotions just won't stop showing up all over the place.

"Hey, you've cried enough for today. No more Dylan tears, okay?" He smiles at me wiping my tears with a tissue he was holding for just in case I cry and yes

I cried. He knows everything about me, when I am about to cry, when I need a hug, when I need to be scolded and all I wish the whole time is that maybe just maybe if Dylan was somewhere like him, I would've been the happiest I have ever been in my entire life.

I nod and whisper, "Okay."

"It's quite late already, I think you should sleep and I'll probably make a space for myself in this sofa." He smiles a brighter smile this time. I don't know how he found out that I'm probably alone at home, but it's good that he finally came to Texas. This is only the happiest thing that I haven't lost until now. Ethan's love. He loves me more than anything that he treasures in his life after his parents and I still wish that Dylan would be the same.

I climb the stairs and as soon as I get in, the doorbell rings.

"I'll take that!" Ethan screams, but I don't want him to open it. Mom might have sent some relatives over for my protection. So, thinking about that I jog to the living room, but right at the moment, Ethan opens it and I hear him talking softly.

What's going on here?

Ethan walks out the door, leaving the door slightly open and after a few seconds I hear two male voices. One's Ethan and the other one, I'm not even sure. I don't want to be sure, but I still try to listen to what they are huffing about.

"Crap, just once I said!"

"The sight of her crying alone awfully in her room is extremely horrifying; you sure don't want to witness that scene." Ethan speaks for me. He sure is talking about me.

"What? Hey, I'm sorry I hurt your ex-girlfriend but I really think I need to apologize to her. I was very rude and I realize it now." He almost yells.

"What is it?" I walk in the conversation between the two men's that I have loved the most after my betrayal father.

"Hi Stella, I'm... I'm extremely sorry. For everything." And just listening to his voice makes me weak like a feather.

After all these weeks of trying to forget him, the results crystal clear.

"What are you on about?" I try not to make any eye contact, not to make any mistakes by letting him know how weak I can be.

"Look, I care about you which is why I have to let you go. I can't hurt you any longer." He speaks up a lie, a complete fatal lie.

"You care about me? Bullshit!" I yell this time, I have to. I want to tell him how much he has hurt me and how less this words prick compared to all the crap he has given me to step on to.

"I don't know what to do to make you realize that I do, but I just don't think that I'm in love with you. And that was why I thought we should just keep our distance until you realize that you're done with your feelings for good. Earlier I called to make sure of it, if you were okay now. I'm sorry, but I just don't want to feel guilty anymore of hurting you so much. I've never loved anyone and I don't think I can, either. So, I want to tell you that I'm not choosing someone else over you. This is just me, I hurt people and I'm not good at any other thing. I want to change that for now, I want to talk to you. I like talking to you, spending time with you, acting all crazy. I'm sorry for all these bullshit, but I want to know if you're done with the hatred towards me. That's it." He sighs after his explanation for coming to my place. I think I know everything about what he just mentioned, but I have no words to share.

I look at Ethan to help me out and he does. He walks past me to answer Dylan and slowly whispers, "She never recovered, not even close."

I turn around to not let Dylan see me, my tears.

I slowly walk inside my house to my room thinking about everything Dylan said tonight. I know for a fact that he doesn't think he deserves some shit but that doesn't mean he should blindfold himself to see the truth around him. I'm in love with him like any other high schoolers and I would do anything to prove him wrong that he deserves love, he deserves some affection. If not from me then at least from someone who loves him truly.

Dylan, even though I have this insecurity called *thantophobia*, (i.e. A phobia of losing someone you love) I would still choose to spend some time with you. Because I know that I will lose the people around me and yes, I wouldn't regret falling in love with you. I am and will always support you. And for the record, I know I'm insane. I should never forgive him, but that's what people call love, don't they? We keep forgiving one another for the heck of it.

"Stella! Stella!" Ethan comes running upstairs to my room as I constantly hear his loud and wide footsteps I start getting annoyed. As soon as I see him right next to my door and about to enter, I close my eyes and look away. The door makes a huge shutting sound and I open my eyes wide to find myself doing magic.

I just did something mom told me not to. I take a deep breath and try to control my annoyance and anger, I suppose. I close my eyes and once again try to remember everything about my horrific past with Dylan but I fail. I still can't remember it all. I can't feel anything for him even though I know that I was shattered many times because of him and I still don't know why I cry sometimes whenever I see him or talk about him. Is it my past crying or is it just the realization of the new me that is rejuvenating and failing at the same time? As they saying goes, 'memories keep us alive' but for me it works exactly the opposite, I've died a thousandth and Dylan hasn't witnessed a single death of me. I know that I was pathetically in love but I do hope that he does, I hope he does go through the same death that I went through. And I'll definitely make sure of that. I open my eyes and I see Dylan leaving through the main gate from my window. The only person I was waiting for to apologize over and again to me for what he has done in the past, I don't know why but I'm still not satisfied with his kindness. He tries his best to be kind but he somehow always puts me down.

Why did you come? I whisper to myself into the thin chilly air knowing the fact that Dylan would never hear my words.

He stops and turns around to look at me standing near my window. He stares the longest stare with his beautiful eyes, trembling legs and face full of guilt. I hear his voice under his throat, inside my mind echoing out loud, maybe the words I want to hear from him. The ones I would never get to hear.

> *I'm sorry, Stella. I know I've hurt you too much for an apology like this, but I want to make sure that I haven't at least turned you to someone else. My confused feelings have been troubling you for too long now. You know even if I chose someone else on top of you, I'd still be there for you. I'd always find my way back to you and I hope to see you as the same beautiful headstrong person like you were before me, before I crumbled down your world. I really hope I get to witness your old-self again.*

He then leaves without a single word spoken. I leave the guest room where Ethan will be sleeping tonight. I assure him that I'm fine, will be fine. As I keep thinking of Dylan, I clear out the puzzle of the day. I hugged him in school once when I figured that dad was betraying me for over 5 years or so and Dylan was there for me when nobody else was. How could I not remember that Dylan held me then?

Right after half an hour when I suppose that Dylan has reached his home already, I receive a text. I read the notification on my phone screen and it says Dylan. A sudden rapid heartbeat comes and leaves the second I whisper his name in the hallways. I could still smell his body scent next to our hallway door where he was standing and as I read along the text while walking, every single word I read through just struck me. This astonishment does not end until I enter my room and climb to my bed reading the text over and over again for the 50th time, just trying to make sure if I got the right text and if it isn't me imagining.

> *"I'm sorry, Stella. I know I've hurt you too much for an apology like this, but I want to make sure that I haven't at least turned you to someone else. My confused feelings have been troubling you*

for too long now. You know even if I chose someone else on top of you, I'd still be there for you. I'd always find my way back to you and I hope to see you as the same beautiful headstrong person like you were before me, before I crumbled down your world. I really hope I get to witness your old-self again."

-Dylan

What on Earth is happening to me now?

CHAPTER 16

A little too hard for everyone

"Yeah, he was here."

"Wasn't it a really good idea to see Ethan again?" Mom smiles brightly showing all her teeth and gums in addition.

"Ouch!" I squeak with a very delightful feminine voice as my pinky finger snaps to the suitcase's handle.

"Honey, you okay?" Mom hurries dropping the handbag she was carrying.

"I'm fine, mom. Don't overreact." I kiss my pinky as she giggles remembering how I pretend like I am all strong like a man.

"I missed you." She whispers, pulling me in a tight hug.

"I missed you too mom. Now snap out of this senti- typical TV show's mom, please." I bend over to lift the suitcase and pull out the handle again, this time being more careful.

"Thank you for being so obedient and honest." She smiles at me with a tilted head. She's never going to change, is she?

"I meant for not doing magic even when you're hurt and I love you for that. If I were you, I would do magic every single second I find myself in a difficult situation. But honey, I don't want you to hide your emotions from your mom. It's okay to cry." She takes a few steps towards the stair carrying the handbag again with flowers in her free hand.

"Mom.." I whisper, but she doesn't hear me.

"Aren't you coming?" She turns around with a worried face this time.

"I am."

I know she's right, I have to cry and let go of everything that's causing me pain inside.

I need to see dad.

"That.. might not be the best choice." Mom looks at me, dropping the boxes on top of her study table.

"Mom, what's why my special power?" I ask her again.

"You don't need to rush. It's going to take time for you to realize what you got inside yourself. You are too disturbed right now because of.. you know who I'm talking about." she walks forward and grabs my hand.

Her warm touch of a mother never fails to surprise me by its never ending love.

"I know mom but at this point of my life, the only person I think can help me is dad. I'm sorry but it's my last hope." I pull back my hand, hurting her inside but she tries to hide her emotions.

"I have no grudge over your father for what he did or has been doing, but I just want you to think it over. That's all."

"Mom asked you to come?" I look at him, astonished.

"That's true." Dad says softly, thinking why she asked him to meet their daughter who he abandoned.

"It's okay; I don't want to hate you right now." I tell him as I have some mother skills of reading mind too.

"What did you want to know or ask?" He questions me strangely like a.. stranger. That's how strong our father- daughter bond was for all this time, like a complete stranger.

"I'm sorry; you probably might be really busy as you just got married and all." I try to lighten up the air by smiling at him after years.

"Indeed, but a little time to spare for my daughter's concern is not a problem to me or my *lovely* wife." He smiles.

"I'm happy for you." I smile at him, a fake smile.

"You really don't have to do that. I know what it's like to lose something." he looks around the home, trying to remember his happy moments with mom and the little me.

We lost you dad, I wanted to say it to him, but I don't want to because he already knows.

"I wanted to know how you got over mom." I ask him, finally.

"Uh.. pardon me?" He stumbles.

"You heard it right." I look confident this time, ready to learn my father's tactic ways of unfaithful love in the world as hateful as this.

"I.. I never got over your mom. She's beautiful and I could never find any reason to leave her behind, ever." He speaks truthfully.

"I know she is, I can't think of any too." I smile.

"We were having problems when she was pregnant with you. I wanted to work for the family that was coming by after your birth. I used to come home late after work and she thought something was not right. She wanted me to spend most of my time with her, but I didn't want to. I wanted to earn and be stable enough for you to never have any complaints against our upbringing of you. It turned out the opposite. I met *her* then when I was all shattered in the dark as we had an argument again. I was in the park and *she* was like a saver to me. I don't like doing magic like how your mom used to when she was a little girl. I didn't like the magic world like she did. We were respected as being one the most powerful families and I think that's what brought *this woman* to my life, for a change. I'm sure a lot of people cursed our family as we were having a wonderful child coming on her way. Somehow, I fell in love with this woman the very moment I laid my eyes on *her*; *she* seemed so soft yet so powerful. *She* was the first women who made my eyes fill with tears and that's not normal for a wizard, especially if it's a man."

"So, you were in love with that lady even after my birth, for six months." I feel pushed away like I was nothing important to him, then. I was abandoned by my own father.

"Don't take it the wrong way; feelings don't change by our will. I tried but I was helpless. It's the only weak point for a wizard, *love*." He whispers the last word.

"We can ignore it but never forget. Not seeing her was killing me inside." He surrenders. That's exactly how I feel.

"What if I tell you that I'm going through the same pain?" I look at him and throw a glass of water on the floor with my power as soon as I turn towards it.

"You're too young for a love like that." He looks at me in the eye and I feel like it is ineffective. He lifts his arms and puts back the glass back in its place.

"I can't stop thinking about him, what do you call this?" I ask him, embarrassed and turn away.

"It's young love. I don't want you to be in it for any longer. I'm sure the Devils planned this, to make you fall in love with a... human." He walks closer to me but I walk away.

Wizard, magic, love, human, memory and now devils. How am I supposed to live a normal life? Why can't I love a human? What is so bad about being born as a wizard that I get punished for being with a human? Why does everyone force me to do what they want and not think about what I actually want?

I leave my home and go to, I don't even know where. I pull out my keys from my jacket because winter is finally back, with all the chills and cold weather entering into my life.

It's been almost a week now. Save me, Lord.

I walk down the road, crossing the same bar again. I miss him, but I shouldn't. I shouldn't be overreacting; I should have listened to Dad and what he was trying to explain. I'm sure he has a better solution than no solution.

I stand in front of the tree that's been here since I wonder how long, centuries probably. After thinking about my decision for the tenth time, I decide to finally call up Dad.

"Hey, I'm sorry for that." I sigh.

"It's totally okay, I've been there before." *Sure.* I roll my eyes and see some of Chloe's friends passing by and we wave at each other, me giving the brightest smile that I have given this entire year so far.

"I want to know how you *stopped liking mom?*" I ask him, more like an order.

"Yeah, that's what I was telling you." He sounds sad.

"Yeah, and I would like you to skip out all the details." I come out honestly, hoping he would understand. While this time I see some couple from my school that I didn't expect to be dating.

Well, because smart people are not supposed to be dating. Duh.

"Like I said, I never stopped liking your mother. It's just that we all love someone way too much." He says, with a confident mind.

"I always loved her, but I have been just, not in love with her anymore because of all the turmoil in the family, in us." He continues. I close my eyes and listen to his shaky voice.

"I fell in love with another person and I couldn't stop it either way. Life made me choose and I chose your mother but we were never happy anymore for a long term. She understood." He opens the cap of a bottle and takes in a gulp of water down his dry throat. I can feel his nervousness through his breathing. Tears creep down my eyes and I let it share its warmth to my cheeks.

"Thanks dad." I end the call and decide to finally get a life.

I get into my car and start driving as I make another call.

"Isaac, can I see you? Right now"

"So what if there's a girl, who likes a guy her closest friend used to have a huge crush on. She first started off hating him because of her close friend but as time passed by, she realized that she was actually starting to have some feelings for him. They started conversing as they had a lot of mutual friends and you know parties and all. He later found out that she liked him, but then she thinks that he likes someone else and that he is not the right guy for her. Actually, her best friends told her that he's not worth her tears and they are right. Even he said that he isn't worth her and she can't forget him at all. What do you think is the best thing the girl should do in order to forget him, totally?" I take a deep breath in and leave it out. Yup calling up Isaac and asking for some love advices was what I meant by getting my life sorted, not.

"Why does she need to forget him in the first case?" Isaac asks with his eyebrow high like a mountain, he just did his eyebrow a couple of days back so he's just showing them off.

"Because he's a-"

"-Major coward?" Isaac completes my line which I wasn't expecting him to say, but somehow similar to what I was planning to say. A coward, that's all he is.

"Uh, yeah." I check my phone as I get a notification. Random shares.

"Reasons are firstly, because he doesn't realize how much she likes him and how lucky he is to have someone to look after him despite all his reckless decisions over life. Secondly, no one else can love him as much as she does and he clearly does not realize that. Thirdly, he doesn't know the meaning of love. How cowardly of that guy to be such a coward." Isaac judges Dylan as if he already knows who the guy is.

"Okay, yeah, but he's a nice guy." I defend the bloody Dylan.

"Stella, why don't you just quit trying to hide it?" Isaac takes a sip of the Latte he ordered.

"Hide what?" I ask him rolling my eyes.

"The fact that you're in love with Dylan and you can do nothing to stop it." he knows. Crap, all I wanted to hear.

"Okay, I've been talking about Dylan the entire day and it's freaking me out because he's coming back in what, 40 hours?" I raise my eyebrows, lift my right leg and place it on top of the left to sit cross-legged.

"You can't stop it okay? Just wait for him. I'm sure he likes you back." He winks.

"Don't dare you wink at me again." I give him an evil look as we laugh together.

"But really, I can't always be this hopeless. I need to move on and you know Dylan, he's just him."

"So, why are you here?" Isaac asks.

"I want answers." I look at him in the eye and smile.

"Have you ever looked into the eyes of someone you loved and realized the person you know is gone?" Isaac looks serious enough making sure that he sounds all deep and broken.

"Oh, shut up, you. I've heard this line many times. It's pretty famous." I laugh it out.

"I'm asking you." Isaac is serious.

I think about the question again and repeat it in my mind many times. The answer clearly does not change.

"Yeah." I smile.

"Me too." he smiles back looking straight into my eye and we finish our drink talking about school starting after three days.

"I'm tired."

"Of?" He asks.

"Dylan." I whisper and all he does is smile like an idiot.

"Then just forget him. Erase *all* the good memories." Isaac laughs jokingly.

"Yeah, I should." I giggle but honestly.

I want to forget him, *again*. I don't want to remember the things about him that made me like him anymore. I don't want the memories to come back at me and hunt me down until I drown into my own shadows filled with a void.

Save me some tranquil at the end, at least. Let him be done and gone from my life, forever.

CHAPTER 17

No one knew

Sydney comes to see me for dinner and what she tells me, turns to be divinely surprising. As we walk to my room, we talk about universities.

"You can leave this city for a while, a year or two. Start your new life in an amazing place; it's going to be full of surprises. We've all graduated already anyways and you can take your major at London as well. I have friends who study there and they said its fun there. I mean well, who doesn't love London?!" She sounds so cheerful, like always.

"Thanks Sydney, I need to ask my mom about it and I'm pretty sure she won't like the idea of me leaving her alone for years." We enter my room and sit on top of my bed. Mom will be back next week and I'll probably ask mom then, hopefully.

"Dude, you are eighteen already! You can do as you want and go where you like. It's your life, enjoy it until you have it." She knows how stressful, it's been for the last few months since Dylan came back, my parents got a divorce finally and dad's expecting his new baby in about seven months as well. I've never seen mom this upset and seeing me every day is a torture for her and myself as I can do nothing to end her sorrow.

Grace will come to live with mom after three months, according to mom's lawyer and I finished my high school last week. I haven't spoken to anyone since.

I think I need it, a long break.

I will not be back for three years at least and I'll meet new people there. Everything will get better.

"Um, yeah. I think I will go to London." I smile at Sydney.

"Well, that's amazing! That calls for a major party!" She screams.

"No, I'm fine with just a dinner. I don't want something loud and huge." I smile at her and cough a little as I've not been feeling well for few days now.

"Oh okay, as you wish Stella." She hugs me tightly, "Ugh! You're finally leaving, you are so lucky. My parents won't let me leave this town ever for a million years." She puts up a sad face and laugh because yes, her parents are of 80's. But my parents aren't the best parents as well. I can't even call them parents, divorced parents.

I'm not sure if I should tell my mom or not about me moving far away. She might be scared of me misusing magic and all but I will try my best to hide my identity.

"So, I'll be leaving now. Thank you for the dinner and I will definitely come to your dinner party." She winks at me and gets off the bed.

She kind of had a thing for Dylan before, but I'm not sure about now, she's probably done with him.

I walk her to her car and say our goodbyes. I have a feeling that I'll see Sydney more often than I need to. She's been looking after me a lot for a while.

I start writing letters today.

For mom, Grace, my friends, dad, Dylan.. I'm not sure about that. I planned on leaving without telling anyone. So, basically sneaking out from the country. No one will know about it except for Dylan because I had to tell him that I'm leaving soon to somewhere. I just wasn't sure that it would be out of this country, so far that no one can ever reach me.

I'll give these to Sydney as she's the only person who knows where I'm going and with whom, her cousin.

As I've known that being a wizard is very beneficial, I could just make thousands of notes from a hundred dollar note and I did. I transferred tons of money to my bank account, transferred some from mom's which she'll never have any idea of and moreover, I sold all my designer bags. According to the amount of money I have, I'm pretty sure it will last for more than just five years of university and more. If it's not enough then I can get a job as well, I've applied for seven universities there which is definitely hard but easy with magic as I moved all my admission dates to four months back. No one will ever have any clue about it.

I hear a doorbell and I run from all the way from my room as I've never been this excited for something and open the door with a wide smile.

I see dad standing in front of me.

"Hey, dad." I breathe out.

"Are you planning to leave to somewhere?" He asks me; how did he even know?

"No, why would I?" I act normal and invite him in.

"I'm not here to sit Stella. I heard you're moving to somewhere, is that true?" He asks with a grin.

"I just said no." I put my right palm on my hip and stare at him.

"If you're trying to run away from your fears and feelings, this is definitely not the best choice." By now I can tell that he's pretty sure about what he's talking about and he won't listen to me.

"Okay, thanks. Then, can you help me with forgetting him?" I ask him annoyed because he can't do shit about it.

"Yes." He says confidently.

"You do?" I whisper this time looking into his eyes and trying to listen to what he is thinking.

"Yes." He repeats, again. He is not thinking at all, he is telling the truth.
"He.. How?"
"Erasing memory is the only way."

"Again?" I ask him because I know that when one day I realize that my memories were erased, it'll haunt me down and I know the feeling of the desperate need of wanting to know every detail of it. I've experienced it just recently and I'm not sure if I'm ready to face another.

I close my eyes and think of Dylan. I don't want to erase him when I already did once. I really don't but he leaves me no choice.

*Flashback- Five months back *

It's been a month since school started again, more like since Dylan came back.

I haven't talked to him all along, but today is a different day.

Hi Stella, hopefully you remember me this time." He smiles as soon as he figures that we are the only one on third floor and we are just standing two lockers apart.

"Nah, I do." I smile back pleasantly.

"I wanted to ask you.. I mean.. It's been a few days since I've been thinking.. to ask you.. I mean only if you want.. If we can.. I mean.. Talk about our math homework? Study together?"

"Sure, when?"
"Like, today?"

"Um.. I need to ask my mom for permission." I walk two steps away from him, facing the other side.

One ring.. Two rings.. Three rings.. Four rings.. Fi-
"Yeah?" My mom asks.

"Mom, should I.. Go practice Math with Dylan?" I ask her because I literally have no idea of what I should be doing right now.

"Oh? That's a turn of events which I was expecting. Just don't stay too late." I can feel that she's smiling on the other end of the line but somewhere she's worried for me.

"Yes, mom." I hang up.
"So?" Dylan asks from right behind me as I shriek a bit.
"Okay." I nod.

He smiles and walks fast, leading us to the school exit as I slowly with magic, close the door of one of the classes that was left open because I'm just that excited. We walk down the stairs and it's a very good day because no one at school has noticed us together, kind of.

"So where are we heading?" I break the silence.
"There's a restaurant I want you to see."

After we reached the restaurant and parked his car next to a big truck, we walk in together.

"Do you remember?" He asks.

"What?" I look around and there are a few people having pastas, drinks and coffees. One of the waitresses smiles at us as if she knew us. What am I supposed to remember in this place?

"What about this?" He pulls me to the table to the right corner of the restaurant which seemed pretty cozy. There is a painting hanging on the wall that seemed quite old and expensive.

"What are you talking about?" I ask him one more time.

"What about this?" He asked again one last time, holding my hands and pulling it to his chest right after. I pull my hands away the very moment.

"What're you doing?" I ask him because it was very weird of him doing all these.

He looks into my eyes as if he is searching for something, wanting to catch a memory of us somewhere deep down inside me, trying to pull it all, "Stella, this is where I asked you out for the first time." He whispers in the thin air.

And I keep staring at him.

Flashback ends

As I walk down the street, I see an old man carrying a bag full of groceries for his young granddaughter. He is worried about her school fees because his son is a lousy alcohol drinker who hasn't paid his daughter's fee for months now. His wife is uneducated and earning money by selling street garbage's every day in the recycle shop. This old man is worried about how he might die anytime and he doesn't want to, only for his granddaughter and his daughter in law. They are both beautiful and he doesn't want to leave them by themselves. While crossing the road on the green light, he wishes to make it to his home alive today to see his wonderful family.

If I were him, I would wish to die than to witness my unhappy living off garbage family but this is life. Life's all about money, struggle, pain, sorrow and for the most part love, that's what keeps us all going.

I keep walking down the market and see a little girl holding his father's hand, she wants a Barbie that she saw yesterday, but she's scared that her teddy bear might eat her while she's asleep. She's scared that her beautiful Barbie might be dead the next morning; she's scared that her Barbie might never wake up after that. She knows that if she tells her father to buy the doll, he won't hesitate because they have enough money but she doesn't want her Barbie to die. So, she leaves a small smile on her face and gives up on her Barbie in the end because that's how much she can do for her.

How hard must it have been for her to leave the Barbie behind?

She's like me, in a world unnatural as this, I'm scared of the bad teddy bear to break me apart from my Barbie. Why has the world come to this? Why is there racial discrimination, gender inequality, drug addicts, murderers, serial killers, human rights violation, I just don't get why. We have this one life and why are we wasting it on something so unlike ourselves just to praise the hell's God to pull us down there? Why should I run, from my family, my friends, my love?

Why can't I just be happy with a human and forget about being a wizard. Why is it so hard?

And I remember Dylan thinking, "I wish I could tell you that I don't want you to leave and I want you to stay here, with me and everyone."

He could never say it upfront, but he always had it in his mind. We loved it each other and no one knew.

But I have to leave because I can't remember any of it to make me stay.

CHAPTER 18

A new beginning

'I am a very uptight trustworthy girl named Stella, 18 years old. I like playing soccer and badminton. I study in an art school in Maple Cross, London.' I drop my pen after I fill my application form for community service and I sign it on the bottom of the page where it says to. I pack my school bag, pat some winter cream on my face, pull-up my hair making a bun and smile at the mirror to myself which is a very weird thing to do every single day.

I slowly walk to my school meeting my sister half way through the road as she takes her regular bus she always does. I'm turning 19 in a couple of months and I'm graduating right after and I'll make my last months the best of my life. I am joining an art school in London for a year and then I'll start getting more into fashion designing for university. As we open our locker we see pretty girls dragging their feet towards us giggling and talking aloud, making everyone around us look at them. They were Emma, Daisy and Chloe, my best friends and yes they are all extremely beautiful, awkward that I never really mentioned them being nosy to anyone. I smile at them as we exchange our morning greetings and hugs like an adult.

"Stella, did you write something in the class report?" Emma asks me sarcastically. The last thing I wanted to hear this early in the morning. Chloe gives a bad glare to Emma. I pretend like I do not really care when I actually spent my entire night yesterday thinking about what to write for my final essay, "Family and their importance in the novel?"

Daisy walks closer to me and regretfully says "I wish I could get that topic. I can't write anything about the society thing. I am all blank!"

I smile at Daisy and give her a sorry face when Emma asks again, "Stella! Did you even start?"

"Why do you even bother?" I ask her rudely not wanting to hear any more from her as I pull my Chemistry book out of my shelf, lock my locker and wrap the book in my arms.

"I was just wondering what you would write." Emma looks annoyed yet smirks giving me goosebumps all over my body. Emma and I are not good terms right now. Even though we have always been best friends, she holds a grudge against Madeline for she liked Dylan and tried to come between us. I argued with Emma about it for not talking to Madeline because Madeline is a nice girl after all.

We slowly walk towards our first period class when Chloe interferes, "That's some kind of bullshit to ask, Emma. At least not this early in the morning." Chloe does not like Emma much for the way Emma has started to backfire me from the group since few weeks. I envy Chloe for her effort.

"What's your problem?" Emma looks annoyed again. I just don't get why she hates me.

Daisy breaks her silence, "Guys, I'm going library to do some research on my topic."

Chloe smiles at her, "Yeah, go ahead. We will catch up with you later" and facing towards Emma, "and you better be careful with what you speak."

Emma raises her eyebrows to her best friend, "Quite threatening, huh?"

Chloe leaves a short air from her nose, "Yeah, you can take it as you want or just jot it down."

Emma scrunches her nose, "Okay boss, I'm not a kid."

Chloe rolls her eyes, "God knows." And she leaves a sigh.

I interrupt them, "It would be better if you guys stop this topic here. The boys are here."

Emma starts naming them, "Oh! It's Dave, Dylan, Elijah, Carter and wait who is the new face? I've never seen him in town." We all turn around to look at our friends. Yeah, we love them.

"Hey girls, what's up?" Elijah asks as we all stop staring at the new guy.

Chloe smiles, "It's the same old stupid-" And as I realize that she is going to talk about Emma, I break in between looking at the guy I don't have any clue about, "Who are you?"

Dave comes forward to answer me as he rubs his palms to one another, "Zack! New in town, here for a few months, live next to my place and fortunately my cousin!"

Zack smiles and answer my question, "Hey, that was a lot for who are you" Making everyone giggle and it changes the atmosphere between Emma and Chloe a bit.

End of Stella's Point Of View

Stella looks at everyone and then turn back to Zack, "Not at all, you might be kidding me. I would love to know a lot more about you." And she smiles at him faintly.

Zack and Stella slowly start asking each other about one another and walk past the group.

Carter whispers, "She is a fish, I tell you guys."

Dave screams dramatically, "Darn, not to my cousin! I don't think she would try though." And he looks at the way Stella and Zack left and laughs.

Chloe, "She's just fooling around. She'll be good to him."

Emma looks at Carter, "Maybe, but I am good with Dylan and anyways she is just used to it, going for random guys. Such a cheap little girl."

"You guys! I don't understand you! Best friends always up to something." Chloe says, looking at Emma and Carter.

Emma speaks harshly, but in a girly manner at the same time, "Whatsoever! You never fell for someone, did you? That's the reason you don't understand us. Go get a life, Chloe stop defending Stella and hiding away her flaws!"

Chloe stares at Emma for a while and left the group and Paul whispered in Emma's ear, "That was rude."

Emma gets furious, "Rude my feet! She always stands next to Stella, don't you see?"

Stella went to see Chloe after knowing what happened and what Emma said to her. Then Chloe asked for a promise from Stella, a promise to never fall for someone who is not worth her. Stella didn't think much and agreed with Chloe. Chloe was more than just a best friend for Stella. Stella's friends meant the world to her. She was someone pretty, nice, perfect and Emma could never resist her beauty. Although there was nothing so great either, in both their life but lots of things changed and happened when time passed.

Stella screamed the moment she got to Chloe's house, "Wow! It's already been a year you got married and I'm here just now! I am so sorry. When did you first meet though? I never got to hear the story!"

Chloe smiled, "It is okay. It's a big world anyway. Well, we met after I graduated."

The atmosphere in Chloe's house was great. There were all friends around laughing and enjoying the first anniversary. There were noises and laughter all around the rooms. Stella could recognize some of the ladies present there, they were from her high school and the rest who weren't Chloe introduced them to Stella. Stella was happy knowing new people and seeing old friends, life seemed nice for a few hours at Chloe's party unless Stella asked something very different which made everyone in the houses silent. Stella rubbed an old wound that was healed a long time ago. She asked aloud, "Where is Emma?"

It seemed like everyone knew about her. No one spoke for twenty seconds, but stared at Stella. Chloe then cleared her voice; kept the wine glass she was holding on the table, "She is no more…"

Stella's eyes widened and she could not believe Chloe's words, she smiled unbelievingly and asked again, "What do you mean by that?" Chloe repeated herself again, "She is gone, Stella."

Then Stella understood a little. She asked curiously, "what happened? How did I ever not know about it?"

"She had a cancer, last stage. She was hiding it from all till she had only a few weeks left. She didn't want to hurt you Stella." Chloe sadly said.

Stella was startled, "But if all of you knew about it and was hurt, why me… not to bear? Why is it only me to not get hurt?"

Chloe looked around to everyone and said, "I am sorry guys. Guess the party is over."

Everyone could understand the situation and all of them quietly moved on. Stella's eyes were full of tears. She couldn't bear what she heard. Then Chloe explained her everything that have happened once upon a time. Chloe said, "You know, I always thought Emma was stupid and mean. I thought she never cared about you but she did care for you Stella. She loved you more anyone of us did. She didn't want you, me or anyone else to realize that."

Stella's eyes were full of tears, she could not bear what she heard and she asked again, "But why?"

Chloe replied, "Her boyfriend was madly in love with you! Her best friend too. She could not bear losing them. She dated Dylan after you left. None of us knew that she liked him. You were- you were so beautifully made Stella that no one could see your little crazy stuffs. Dylan, Nathan, Zack all of them liked you! You were like an extraordinary crystal for them. Emma didn't want to lose Dylan, not unless she found out she was dying. She had hurt you enough and she didn't want to hurt you more. She agreed that she was greedy and jealous, but at her last days, everyone was with her. It's been so hard for everyone to forget her. Years after years-"

Stella broke in again, "Years after years? Exactly how many years have passed since she died?!" Stella knew nothing, Chloe could tell by looking at her eyes and then she continued, "It's been ten years, Stella."

Stella couldn't believe her ears after all she heard was not enough to bear already. She couldn't speak a word. She couldn't blame anyone, but herself for not knowing anything that was going on. There was a grimace of pain in the room. She couldn't believe how she didn't have any clue in ten years? She had come back to her hometown after eleven hard years of working in someone else's country and the first thing she hears is her friend's death. She earned so much for herself to get a luxurious life that she was unaware of the situation with her friends.

Then Chloe interrupted and tried to change the atmosphere, "So? No man in your life?"

Stella thought deeply for a while and realized she didn't have any clue. She knew she was single, but something forced her from within, she couldn't understand what it was but she spoke, "You told me to never fall in love, didn't you?"

Chloe looked astonished, "What?" Then Stella smiled and said," You had my word, Chloe. I couldn't fall for any men."

Chloe screamed, "Not until now! I thought you were getting wealthier, happier and stronger there with someone there!"

"Yeah, I was getting wealthier, stronger and happier. I gave my entire time to work. I enjoyed earning, shopping and official meetings. I became independent and it's all because of you. How my eleven years flew in a blink and I didn't even know, I still feel unaware of what happened with my life all these years." Stella smiled and ended.

"I never thought you would be this way. Hey and do you know that Dylan is still single?" Chloe said and Stella asked, "So what?"

Chloe stepped forward and held Stella's right hand and covered it with her warm hands, speaking softly, "He still loves you and Emma equally. He could never change the feeling he had for you. I always discouraged him for his affection and love he has for you, but right now I want you guys to be one."

Stella pushed Chloe's hand away from hers and couldn't accept the words Chloe said to her and she continued, "I don't want you to be alone because of me."

Stella happily said, "Thank you, but I am sorry to say I don't want to do much more bad deeds. I have done and had enough, it already. Please forgive me for this."

Stella couldn't hurt anyone anymore because of her and she still had to see her sick mother. Chloe knew what was going on but she tried to convince her softly, "Just once Stella. If you go see Dylan, maybe it could change your mind. You are 30 and Dylan is 31, if a week ago I wouldn't have sent you the message about your mother. No wonder if I would be able to see you after ten years more! You would turn 40 and Dylan 42! Can't you see that Dylan needs you? You guys are meant to be together."

Stella didn't speak a word, she was still with her decision and Chloe said again, "I know you since you were fifteen years old. You were born with love and you grew up getting love from everyone around and now I'm telling you it's your turn to show love, give love to someone who needs you and you know who it is without any doubt.

"No! I can't love someone. My love for my people is a curse! I was born with a curse! My dad cheated on me and my mom the moment I stepped into this world. Mother thinks I am a bad luck for the family and she always made me feel like I am the luckiest. My elder brother who I had no clue about lost his legs to save me when I was trying to suicide at eight. Emma, Daisy, Dylan, are the ones I know since I first came to this city and now all I hear that Emma's gone, Dylan's still hoping for nothing and I have no idea where Daisy is. All I have now is my sick mother and my sister."

"Well, I heard Grace's boyfriend lives with her. She has a good life, Stella." Chloe tried to cool her down and sat on the couch finally relaxing a bit. Then Stella calmly continued after a few seconds of deep thinking, "Yes, she surely does have a life. I've been here just for a couple of weeks, what do I have to do?" Chloe looked amazed, "What do you mean by that?"

Stella was ready to do anything. She repeated, "What do I have to do for a couple of weeks to make Dylan feel fine and forget all the pain? But- I don't want to get into any relationship with him."

Chloe smiled, she wanted this spirit of Stella and she knew Stella would never let her down for anything and she said boldly, "Do what you can. Break all your promises; make him feel your love again. Do anything and make him alive, not like a living dead that he is right now."

That was all she had to do. For Emma, Dylan and for herself, this world of love was harsh on them, but she would do anything to overcome all the sorrows, pain and sufferings Dylan went through because of her.

Stella headed to her home, she had left behind eleven years back. The same old street, but there was more 100's of houses built by then. Old people selling fruits and vegetables on the market screaming through their vocal chords to earn some pennies brought a smile to Stella's face. They were happy looking at Stella thinking it was Grace. Stella only silently went forward and she could hear many others talking too. She did not speak a word and reached home after fifteen minutes and as soon as she rang the doorbell, within five seconds the door opened wide. There was someone tall, fair, happy and a good looking man there right next to Stella.

The moment she saw him, she came to know that it was her sister's boyfriend. He looked at her astonishingly not yet smiled. He seemed to be around his mid-20, holding a bowl of soup in his hand, his presence made a good impression on her sister's choice. As soon as Stella smelled the soup she found out that it was for someone sick in the house and that would probably be her mother.

Stella then asked him, "Can I?" and then suddenly the man answered with a thick manly voice, "Yes! Sure! Come on in!" He surely seemed like a happy man to Stella. The house was beautiful than it was before, it had a full interior repair. Then a lady like voice asked softly, "Who's there?"

Both Stella and the guy smiled at each other and he said, "It's someone you haven't seen for years, my dear!"

Then he turned to Stella and said, "She'd love to see you." He held her hands softly and took her to a room, a room where Grace used to sleep in before. Stella saw Grace in her bed, lying like a princess covered with a beautiful blanket of furs. She was kept like a queen there.

Slowly Grace opened her eyes widely in shock and their eyes met each other after eleven years, the pair of blue eyes they were inherited from their father's matched again. Their eyes were filled with tears, love, pain and sorrow. Both of them were similar only Grace's boyfriend could see it. Stella ran to her and kneeled on the carpet and asked Grace, "Are you sick? You are totally wrapped up with this blanket!"

Grace smiled and slowly removed the blanket from her and said, "I'm pregnant, Stella."

Stella's eyes widened as she saw her sister's bulging stomach. Stella hurriedly asked, "How- how long?" and the answer came in quickly too from Grace, "Six months."

Stella was happy after a long time and she screamed, "Wow! My little sister's grown so big!"

Then Grace introduced Stella to the guy, "My husband, Alex Fontaine and this is me Grace Campbell Fontaine." and continued looking at Alex, "Alex? This is my sister, Stella Campbell." Stella realized that Grace did not use their father's last name while introducing, probably because he is not a part of their family anymore she thought.

They smiled at each other like they have met for the first time. Stella was happy for her sister and she could see how happy Grace was to have the baby. Then Alex broke the silence, "Who is the youngest among you guys?" Both of them smiled at each other and Stella answered, "She's the older one. She just looks younger because she's always been that cute chick." Alex, "That's unbelievable! She actually looks younger than you!" Grace faintly smiled, "Yes, indeed."

Then Stella went to her mother's room. She was scared to face her mother. Five years... that's what she was thinking. Eleven years is very long. Her heart was beating fast the moment she saw her face. She was 62 by then, but she looked 10 years older than her age. Mother slowly called her, "Gra-" Stella was gone, Stella thought that her mother would never forgive her. She had done enough to hurt her. She left her in the midst of the time and all Stella thought was that her mother would never dare to forgive her. All the way she came back for, was impossible. She whispered to herself what she wanted to tell her mother all these years, "I am sorry mom. Sorry to be someone from your womb."

Stella was sad and her eyes were full of tears, she slowly turned as she found Grace standing there right next to her. Grace looked pretty. Her eyes were glowing, her tender hand touching her belly seemed caring, her hair was black and she looked older than Stella. Stella felt like she has never seen a strong gorgeous women every like her sister. Grace's voice was soft and straight to Stella, "Why did you come back after all this time? It kept me thinking for a while."

Stella couldn't lie to her sister, "For mother." It was the only reason Stella was standing there. She came to her mother and she was pretty sure about it. Grace slowly grabbed her hand and took her to her room. Stella did not have any idea what she was thinking about to do. "Stella? Dad's dead, mom's sick. I'm pregnant, brother is happy with his family, your friends all got married and I want you to tell me if you are too? Do you have someone in your life, Stella?" Grace asked.

"No!" Stella's answer came fast, "I mean... I'm not in a hurry. I am here for mom and Dylan, perhaps; I'll go back after a few weeks. I'll take time to be with mom and if there's no hope, I'll return."

"Dylan?!" Grace asked.

"Yeah, I have to make him feel fine."

"But- he is!" Grace got furious.

Stella shook her head, pulled out a long sweater from her suitcase and left the house.

CHAPTER 19

The final retrouvaille

Stella knocked the door of Dylan's home after reaching to the address Emma gave.

After walking few steps in the empty which was opened by a housekeeper, Stella saw Dylan after a long time.

"How may I help you?" The maid asked.

"Tell him it's Stella." She replied and the maid looked surprised and let her in.

Dylan was sitting at the couch having some coffee and reading the newspaper with interest. Stella was dragging her feet to Dylan hoping that he hadn't changed at all. She then heard a ladylike voice from nowhere, "Why are you scrolling up like you are going to a church? Come on in."

There was a chuckle from her voice and Dylan too. Then Stella saw the women, she wasn't a woman at all she thought, it was a young lady with a bright smile. She looked pretty but less than Stella, her hair was pinned high, legs were long, face jolly, hands looked soft, a loose tee with a short brown pant with a white room slipper. The young lady looked at Stella very carefully from top to bottom and commented on her out -look, "Hey, your belly hasn't grown at all in five months! You look slim and well your beauty is well maintained or managed huh? Did you dye your hair to black?" Stella came to know that the young lady thought she was Grace. After a second when Stella was slightly smiling, Dylan folded his paper and kept on the table; he stood up and stared at Stella. He looked at her belly, which made Stella embarrass going red, she was blushing. Dylan spoke softly, "Didn't think you would ever be here, like a bird you flew and like a bird you are back without a word."

Stella felt like leaving the house as soon as she could, but her feet would not let her go. Her heart wanted to say something, her eyes were hurt seeing him after all these years, and she had goosebumps all over her body. She felt horrible, shattered, guilty and worse at the same time. Dylan knew that it was Stella standing their clueless without a word for him. The maid who opened the door, walked in and whispered in the young lady's ears. After a minute there was only both of them in the room, the girl was gone somewhere else.

Dylan had a pair of dark eyes nearly black; he was good looking as he was once before. He looked tall and thin as ever, his voice was soft and nice to listen to. He was the same guy she was gazing at, when she was in her 16's. By then she was 30. A lady with money and pride, but it was all of no use in front of Dylan. Even he had everything except a good love life he wished to have once upon a time.

"Oh come on! Are we standing staring at each other the whole day now?" Dylan joked.

He giggled and asked Stella to take a seat but she did not hear him so he grabbed her hands and pulled her holding her cold hands. She got rid of his hand as soon as she could. The reaction made Dylan feel awkward and Stella could see it from his face. He acted fine but she knew that deep inside he wasn't. "Why are you here?" He asked.

"I am sorry I left you behind and I think I am back for you." Stella said knowing that she was not hiding anything and she would not.

"Didn't you see I have a lady living with me in this house under the same roof?"

Stella couldn't believe what she heard, "What? She is just anyone..."

Dylan did not seem happy hearing her and he gave back her words to herself, "Not just anyone, a twenty six years old woman is living here."

"Twenty six? But look at her and look at- me?!" Stella stood embarrassed after comparing herself with someone.

"What makes the difference between you and Savannah?" Dylan asked.

"You make difference! What happened to your choice? How.. She?" Stella stammered.

Dylan was angry, "Why are you even telling me this? What will happen if I am with her, Stella?"

He went harsh but he had to, Stella wanted him to be it. Stella was saying things she did not want to and she knew it would only hurt both of them, but she thought maybe just doing it would make them feel better. Hurting one another. Stella then answered, "I am telling this because you are more than that little lady! I care for you. Don't ruin your life!"

"I have already ruined my life once, she changed me, she cares for me a lot and you know the big difference between you two? She loves me and you always made me love you!" Dylan spoke aloud and it was enough for Stella to hear.

"Thanks Dylan, by the way, I am leaving after two weeks. If you have anything to tell me, do call. I will be waiting like I always did." She scribbled numbers on a small paper and left it on the table on top of the paper Dylan was reading earlier.

Stella was leaving the house, but she turned back one last time as she was not satisfied with what she said. She had to tell a truth to him for once and for all, "And a thing to you Mr. Darrington, you make mistakes all this time. I made you love me because I loved you, but you chose Emma not me and there surely is a big difference between that Savannah and me, the only one to know is you."

"Ste-", The door banged in Dylan's face. He was all alone, all by himself after a long time. He realized at that moment that no one ever left him by himself alone and sad in all these years although deep inside he was. He asked to himself, what had happened that he had to choose Emma instead of Stella. How could he ever make that mistake because all he ever knew was that he loved Stella more than Emma? What happened? Why hasn't it ever struck his mind? He never had time to think all of these, but why?

At midnight Dylan called Stella and they planned to see each other the next day for a lunch. It was the same place they would go every time when they were young as eleven years back. Dylan reached earlier and he was standing for 15 minutes, which made him tired.

Stella said "You are ten minutes early." Dylan turned and checked his watch, "It's just five minutes, let's go."

Stella slightly smiled at Dylan and he saw her beauty which would make him fall in love with her once again. She was one of prettiest girl he had ever seen, all the other guys would go crazy for her and Dylan knew that even he was one of them too. It seemed like an illusion to him, seeing her again after all these years of separation.

On the way to the table Dylan thought about it a lot, if he was not late to confess her then they might have been a married couple by then, he was sure they wouldn't break up as he knew she was a wonderful girl that he wouldn't want to lose. She was beautiful, lovely, smart and understanding. As they were eating their favorites they started their conversation by talking about their old days. Everything seemed to be beautiful for Dylan, but there was something wrong in him, Stella realized every time she started telling him something about their days together Dylan just would be in a shock and reply, "Is it? I don't remember any of it! It's been years." And he made many other reasons for not remembering any of it.

Stella was surprised and upset about how he could not remember any of the times they spent together. It was wonderful memories of her. He neither remembered Emma's birthday or Stella's. Those were the dates he would never forget. He had answers to none of Stella's questions. They were together for three hours walking and talking when all of a sudden Dylan said he had to get back home and he would drop Stella on the way. He told he had to take medicine, but for what he did not say. Stella found it weird and asked about the reason for taking medicines, but in vain, she didn't get any answer. Stella was scared with his sudden wild behavior and she agreed to what he said and got into the car. When Dylan started the car Stella could see him trembling, he kicked the car hard as it was not starting. Even though she got terrified she tried to calm him down and suggested to walk. Dylan only sighed and he jumped off the car without any word. They walked for half an hour and Stella could see him shaking for nothing. She wanted to ask and shout at him for his stupid behavior, but she knew it would make the situation worse if she did so. Finally, when they reached his home, he went hurriedly inside, Stella stood outside without a word. After a minute Dylan was out calmly, he looked all fine and good, but this time Stella was not. She had never expected that something like that to happen with Dylan that happened earlier.

"I just don't understand, what is Savannah to you?!" Stella asked in anger.

"She is someone I care for, Stella." Dylan answered to her question. Stella didn't seem happy and she yelled, "Please don't tell me that you love that kid!"

Dylan stepped forward and whispered in her ears, "All the other women will come after you if they find out what you have just said."

Stella did not care for what would happen to her, but at that time all she cared for being Dylan. They were moving forward and yelling at each other as they did not have any intention to make a crowd next to Dylan's door.

"So let them do it! Let them come after me, Dylan! What's the least going to happen? Are you… still the same Dylan?" Stella ended shockingly when she thought about what happened.

"Please! Don't come back in my life! I have Savannah!"

"Why?! She is manipulating you! Can't you see what just happened?" They were crossing the bridge, but something stupid came up again. Dylan looked at her eyes, "If she is doing anything to me, she will. But I can't bear losing you. I don't want you to die like Emma did!"

Stella stopped on the half way holding the grip of the bridge, "Do you know how Emma died?"

"No! I don't know anything!" Dylan's voice rose as if he just woke up.

"But you just said something to me before about it that I cannot clearly remember." Stella stood shocked.

"I don't remember a thing! I don't have any idea what I just said, but please, Stella. Leave me alone here." Dylan turned back and crossed the road.

Stella stepped a foot forward to stop Dylan and ask him about Emma more but someone pushed her backward. Her body turned and flipped back down. She remembered it was a hand that wanted to save her, a force that was trying to protect her as there was a car crossing right through her but she fell down, deeply with the person who saved her. She realized there was water all around her. It was freezing in there and she remembered a few words she was lip-sing.. She was whispering, calling out the name.. Charles.. Charles Stevenson. Charles.. Charles… Emma Block.. Dylan… Charles. She slowly closed her eyes, feeling sleepy in the cold winter water with suffocation, she was suffocating, but it was so cold that she wanted to go deep underground to get some warmth. Her body was all heavy, drowning inside the deep water. She was going down, more down. She could feel the soft touch of fishes running away from her when she came closer to them. She could feel the touch of marine plants. She could remember her past, a dream like a movie screen, she had seen once a long time back. She was young to her 18's again.

CHAPTER 20

The agglomeration of belief

There was Emma, kneeling on the ground with her fist tight to her head; eyes were full with tears and pain. "Emma! Let's just go to the hospital. I am scared seeing you this way all the time!" Stella screamed.

"This.. has to happen, I cannot go to the hospital!" Emma cried.

"Why? You will die with your stubbornness! Please! Listen to me!" Stella screamed at her more.

"Don't worry Stella, I will never leave you. I am meant to live."

"What are you babbling? What do you think the world is? We die anytime, anywhere, anyhow, we will never know…"

Emma was smiling, "The world could stand next to you. I will change everything for you. I swear, I will always-"

Then someone grabbed Stella's waist and brought her up to the surface. She felt warm air. Stella could hear something.

"Please breathe… please… you can't leave me… please breath…" Stella coughed hard, spilling all the water on her face and she could hear the same voice again, "she's breathing! Stella! Stella! Look over! She's alive! I will never let you be alone! I love you."

Stella could see Alex but her vision was a blur. Alex was hugging Grace, Stella slightly smiled, she was happy that her sister had a caring husband like Alex. But... Charles was who she remembered. Who was Charles Stevenson she was preaching for? She was very tired and cold. She slowly closed her eyes to darkness.

"Stella! Stella!" it was Chloe standing there. Stella could see her and asked, "Chloe..where am I?"

"You are brought in the hospital, sleepy head! You slept for fourteen hours. What happened? Heard the accident happened in Brownsville? You went to see Dylan didn't you?"

"Yeah.. but.. I didn't fall by myself, Chloe! Someone else did! Yeah, someone pushed me!" Stella said.

"Hey take a rest. I'll talk to you later, okay? You seem tired." Chloe left the room fast.

Who was it? Stella thought to herself after Chloe left and why didn't Chloe tell me anything? Who would save her life? She felt the hand on her arms, Stella tried harder to remember, but it was all in vain. No one would tell her anything for two days and Stella was discharged from the hospital. When she reached home she saw her mother with eyes full of tears. Stella thought mother had forgiven her for she had caused by then, she thought mother was sorry for her daughter but things were all getting worse.

She heard her mom shout at her, "You should have never returned!"

"Mother!-" Stella shouted too, because she couldn't take it anymore after so many years she had seen her mom and her reaction was not worth any of what she did.

"Get the hell out of here!" her mom shouted at her more even louder. She held her breath. Stella was crying at the moment. Even though she is my mother, how could she be that harsh on me? Stella thought. She could not tolerate anymore from her mother, Suzanne.

Stella whispered, "I am sorry dad, I can't." Stella then apologized calmly to her mother.

"No you aren't! I should have killed you the day I saw your face the first time! You have ruined my Grace's life!" Suzanne screamed.

"Mother, watch it! I am here for good!" Stella responded, feeling like a stranger in her own house.

"No! You ruined my Grace's life! Her womb is empty, you know that? Her baby died because of you!" Suzanne kept blaming Stella but Stella could not understand it.

"Mother you are mistaken. Nothing as such has happened." She said.

"The one who saved you from the accident was Grace and it killed her baby." Suzanne explained and Stella started crying hard, "I can hear and bear anything bad from you mother but never this awful thing! I can't listen to any more of this nonsense. I love my sister and I am sure what you said is not a drop true." Stella said.

"It is and I swear if this is true, you are never stepping your feet in my house or I will kill you! You hear me? I will kill you!" Suzanne lost her balance and turned towards the door.

"Mom! I am fine." Grace said entering the house.

Stella hurriedly turned back and saw her sister, "Grace?" she whispered. She could not express how glad she was to see her sister standing next to the door, "Is your baby fine?"

Grace smiled at Stella, "She's all fine. No need to worry, Stella."

Then Suzanne spoke again, "She is not staying here any longer. I am extremely sorry to say Grace but your child is no more. The reason of her death is this woman next to you." pointing at Stella.

Stella looked at Grace's eyes with lots of hope and she did not let her down, "Mom, you're sadly mistaken for my baby is just gone for a week from now; it'll be back within a week."

"Grace! Honey, please don't tell me you are involved in the magic stuff! Not the Josephs!" Suzanne looked anxious for the first time in years. Grace precisely told her mom without noticing the expression her mother had, "It is the Joseph's mom."

Stella was puzzled, she had not heard of magic for 11 years and all about the Josephs. What was the secret, Stella thought. Then Suzanne spoke again, "You! - Grace?! I kept you so much away from them, but still you are doing irrelevant and risky work for them?" Suzanne was mad at Grace.

Suzanne looked at Grace. Suzanne had so much to tell Grace, so much to lecture, so much to change, teach but she couldn't. Alex held Suzanne to her room and Grace to rest on hers. Stella was alone in the living room with millions of questions running through her mind then after 15-20 minutes Alex entered the hall. Alex sat on the sofa and started to explain her. Stella quietly watched his lips move, hand's move, the face he had. She saw his purity in his language. He really loved his women Stella thought. She felt like she had never seen a devoted man like him and she would never see too. Her sister was lucky to have him, but the words from his mouth made Stella feel uncomfortable about her and her family.

"I am going to tell you a bitter truth. I apologize earlier if you get hurt by my words. It's been six years Grace is trying to stop the Josephs with the help of a member of their family, Chloe is her name. You possibly know her well, but she is locked up as a captive under the tree which lies near the austere, old house at the St. Bill. She has been trying to help Grace. The room Chloe is locked up in is covered by spells which cannot be broken except the older Josephs and none wants to help her. Chloe is fine by herself as she is a wizard herself, she doesn't need to be fed. Another thing, the women Dylan lives with, Suzanne. She is working for the Josephs as she is one of the but fortunately we have a doubt that she is falling in love with him, which is approximately an outstanding and marvelous result we have received after six unbearable years. Which means Dylan can distract that woman any time-"

"Does this all mean that the young lady will be living up with him all his years?" Stella was frustrated.

"You didn't get my point, Ms. Stevenson. This game we are playing is all for you. Grace gave our child's life for you. Earlier, as she was boasting to claim that our child will be in her womb within a week, remember? Well, the possibility if her child to get in her womb is twenty percent only. We are all optimistic here."

"What? You must be kidding me, Alex!" Stella almost screamed.

"You are not a kid to be fooled here, Ms. Stevenson and that is something we both can bet on, can't we?"

"But- why are you calling me Mrs. Stevenson? I am a Campbell, don't you know?"

Stella proudly asks him, but Alex tends to explain her something different than she ever could have imagined, "You are the queen in our chess. We have been protecting you all these years, but it's your turn to make your move and for that you should know how to make the game keep on going swiftly, for which I am here to teach you and explain the rules plus the game reached till now."

CHAPTER 21

The conjuring tricks

Alex went back to Grace's room. Stella was still, totally surprised by what she just heard just before an hour while Grace and Suzanne were screaming at each other but everything changed by then. All her questions were answered. She started thinking hard to herself. She was married. Charles Stevenson was the man she had been living with for three years! The Chloe she met a few days earlier was not her friend; Chloe, but someone from the Josephs pretending to be her who changed her look and made her look like her. Chloe who has been helping Grace is the daughter of Karen Mary, Joseph who is known as the most powerful wizard and was in love with her father. Karen's husband Bob was imprisoned to have killed her father. There were so many things she did not know, but by then Stella knew everything. The last words Alex told Stella were rounding in her mind again and again.

"It's your turn to make a move, think well Stella. You can do anything."

The next day Stella went to the great wizard Karen Mary Joseph's house. "Who's here?" the sharp voice rose up to see Stella and added, "The unwanted stupid Campbell women from London it is. What did you come here for?"

"You know everything about me, but why are you still pretending not to know any?" Stella asked her and anger could be clearly seen in the mother of the Joseph's eyes. Her teeth forced into each other she spoke, "Answer me first!"

"Is my dad dead?" Stella asked. The women held her eyebrows high with rage and power and she replied, "He was dead eleven years ago, didn't you know that?"

"He isn't dead, is he? You are the one who claimed it wrong t the world! You would never kill him!"

"He was dead! Why wouldn't I kill him? I have magic too." She boasted.

"You are jealous towards my mother; you could never bear losing the one you loved. You locked him up somewhere mysterious like you have done to your daughter!"

"What nonsense! Who told you this? Jealous of the Campbell?" Karen laughed.

"Yeah, because the Campbell is special and the Josephs aren't Fontaine! They are older than you are. Just to remind you. We have a Fontaine in our family too! You wanted to kill the little Hybrid! Great plan old lady, but you cannot change the nature!" Stella shouted.

"Campbell and Fontaine? A hybrid? Don't tell me the 32 years Fontaine guy told you all these. He can't preach the rules we serve!" the wizard shouted with fright.

"What rule?" Stella didn't know the world there.

"The first rule! A wizard can never claim themselves to another wizard family member! That's- so just against the law!" Stella laughed hard and asked the wizard if she was scared of breaking the rules.

"We are the high preachers. What do you know about the wizard world? I'm wasting my time, so just come to the point Campbell!" Karen shouted.

"Okay then I want my father back" the wizard looked seriously at Stella and said, "You have a lot of willpower to demand something from me, I appreciate that but unfortunately you won't get him. So better get going home." Then

Karen went in a room and closed the door. Stella was sad she couldn't do anything but leave.

"It's been three hours, why are you still here?" Karen came back as she found Stella still there. Stella seemed tough to Karen. Stella couldn't go back home as it would be shameless to return empty handed, so she thought and looked at Karen and requested, "I beg you to help me. I am not surprised that you know what I am talking about."

"You little! Ugh! What makes you think I'll help you?" Karen asked.

"My father, Edward. You have him so what am I to do when I don't know how to even use the spell?" Stella begged.

"You think I'll teach you magic, huh?" Karen asked.

"No, but my father could, couldn't he? You locked him up because you knew he would teach me the world. You wanted your era to go on, didn't you?" Stella's eyes were full of tears.

"All though I don't want to but just a consideration, kid you did see your father once. It's just that you were an infant and you don't remember. He told you something, he taught you magic. He kept his promise by being by my side. So, I'll keep my promise too. He told me to tell you these and he wanted you to remember it." The lady finished.

Stella thought for a while and asked, "Why did you lock him up for years, then?"

"I never needed to lock him up. He is more powerful than I am, he is immune. Well, it's a promise he made for some reason and he is paying for it." She smiled.

"What promise? Why?" Stella wanted to know so much.

"When you were around seven years old, she would have been in the middle of the road that day during the accident but I didn't let that happen. You were there instead. It's all karma. You were never there to suicide, but every time you were everywhere to save your sister. So, I had to sacrifice your brother instead. I made him see you walking down the street. I had to save you."

"Yeah, 6th September, 1861. Pentagon street 3:21 PM my brother lost his leg because of me, he wanted to save my life. But- why am I unknowingly saving my sister?" Stella asked.

Then Karen looked into Stella's eyes, "Because you have to. The night you were about to come in this world, your father told you to always save your people, your family. I don't want to tell you this, but- you were born with magical powers."

"But- but.. how can I believe you? You tried to kill my family! Alex, Grace, mom everyone told me!"

"If I was never there for you, there would be no family you call yours. I know you are curious, you want to explore everything and I won't disturb you by making riddles and by building them. Edward is with me and no one knows it except you and some of my family members. Your mother is a bad player. She always betrayed your father and your father could not bear it but he could not leave you too. You are right, he is alive." Karen smiled.

"I trust you Karen but I will talk to mother. But please- don't kill my sister's baby. You are the only one who can help me!"

"You know I can only help you and surely will. Just ask your sister the name of the wizard who helped her in removing the soul of the infant. I'll see what I can do then."

"Okay, thank you so much, Karen." Stella was leaving the house when Karen spoke, "just be aware of your mother, you shouldn't be talking to her much and don't tell her about your father's truth."

Karen turned back and went inside a room and Stella went on her way to home. Stella stepped back and went in her room when she reached her home. How could someone say bad about her mother to her face? Stella stepped forward and saw a cup of hot coffee on the table, Suzanne's cup. She lifted the cup and went to Suzanne's room.

"I have to talk to you." Stella told, stretching her hand passing the cup to her mother, but Suzanne rejected the coffee and replied, "But I don't want to."

Stella sighed and placed the cup on the small table and started, "Dad never loved you did he?"

"He did! What do you know about him, you- Whatever!"

"You killed him. Don't you dare lie to me anymore mother!" she wanted to see her mother's anger and wanted to hear the truth about herself.

"Who's talking? You watch out your mouth or I have to tear your tongues apart."

Stella no longer felt afraid of her or sorry or even angry at the women anymore. She lifted the cup of coffee from the table. When she turned to face her mother again, it was as if she had never seen her before. She was a complete stranger. She was a tyrannical, sneaky, boring old woman whom she did not know and did not care to know.

She went to the hall and placed the cup of coffee at the same posture as it was before. It was unbearable to say that the rude liar was her mother. She had had enough of lies and threats. Then she went to Grace's room and saw Grace still with great hope sewing a dress for her coming daughter.

"Stella! I heard you guys screaming. What's wrong? What happened to you?" Grace seemed worried. Stella couldn't speak a word about their mother, although there were so many things she wanted to because she knew Grace wouldn't believe anything about mother for the wrong things. She had to know the name of the wizard who helped Grace then. They gradually asked and answered the question then.

"Grace, who removed the soul out of the baby in the womb?" Stella looked rather solemn. Grace answered with a smile, "Chloe"

"What, don't lie to me!"

"I am not! Chloe is the one who helped me through the room." Grace smiled.

"But how is that even possible?"

"We are using a means of magic to communicate which was used thousands of years back and by how she knows everything that has been going on. The baby is safe with her."

Stella forced her grip towards Grace's arm and tightened, "Didn't you get any other strong or healthy wizard to do so? Her mother will kill her!-"

"No one would help me. Everyone is scared of that old greedy Karen Joseph but I am not and neither is Chloe!" Grace tried to remove Stella's hand away from her arms.

Stella pushed back Grace by leaving the arms. Stella was burning with anger. She couldn't tell Grace how much she cared for her. If Grace would take one wrong step, it would make her kill herself and Stella didn't want that. She would kill herself for her smaller sister. It was the same feeling she had once for her mother but not then. She knew that her mother wasn't a good person and would never be. Stella's eyes were filled with tears, "Karen will kill Chloe if she finds out the truth. If you had hidden your pride and asked Karen for help, she would probably accept it and help you." Stella sadly said and sat on the bed next to Grace.

"No, she wouldn't! Never! Not until I die!"

"Grace! She is helping us and you just didn't have any clue about that, did you?" Stella shouldn't have said that but she had to. The moment the words came out, she regrets it.

"What? She isn't helping us, Stella! She has been fooling you! So, am I wrong again? Go on! Make me say that!"

There was a call from Dylan for Stella and Grace started, "Wow! The old tragic boyfriend again, isn't he?"

"Grace! What's wrong with you? Why are you against me?" Stella stood up and removed her battery from her cell phone and asked her sister again, "What's wrong, Grace? Please I want you to explain."

"I just want you to stay away from Dylan!"

"But- I love him very much. Don't you think that I deserve him?"

"No- Stella, there's someone else waiting for you in London, Charles Stevenson! For god sake, you are a married woman!"

"Wait a minute, Charles Stevenson? I don't know him! Even Alex told me about him."

"Yeah, and he told me how your feelings are ending towards him. You cannot fall in love with Dylan ever again."

"Yeah, I understand, but- why don't I remember him? All I know is he is my husband for three years?" Stella observed her hand and kept staring at her fingers. She did not ever feel like she was wearing a ring.

"What I heard was that you guys don't have a healthy relationship. You guys recently have been quarreling a lot, but still there is a connection between you guy."

"But-" Stella sighed, there were no words left.

After two days when everything was going swiftly. They all had their dinner as the night fell. Stella couldn't sleep and as she closed her eyes, she could vision a world, a dazzling one. She could see Emma again and herself.

"Emma! I have to leave the country soon!"

"Stella, I have an idea. You don't need to worry, don't do anything stupid but.. run away. You know, I have a cousin and he is planning to leave this country for university as well and I'm sure you can go with him, London as we planned. He is all packed and has his family members living there, perhaps an elder sister. If you go then it would be a beautiful place to live and stay away for a while, I'll try to go there too once I convince my parents. What say? Deal?" Sydney asked smiling.

"DEAL!" They laughed together as if they were deciding on something really big.

------------- tsinggggggggggggggggggggggggggggg------------------

Then Stella heard a voice, "Stella! I am having different problems here. I guess something is wrong. Hurry and come to my place we have lots to do."

Stella realized it was Karen in her ears trying to give a message of something wrong. Stella rushed, pulled her warm clothes as the atmosphere was turning colder at night. She borrowed Alex's car to reach Karen's place.

"Stella! We have to start the spell fast. Before the sun rises, before the night falls, before it is five. We are running out of time. Tell the name of the wizard who helped your sister. I need the wizard."

Karen's eyes were glowing and looked sharp. Stella couldn't tell that her own daughter did it. Even the time was running from their hand, but for what? Stella could not find any answer. They only had one more day to accomplish what they could not until now.

"But Karen, what's the rush for? What will happen if the night falls? We have tomorrow." Stella asked.

"No, we don't. Your sister's child will die if we don't do it now. There are certain circumstances of win and lose in magic. The only person who can do this successfully is the person who personally performed it. According to what I am experiencing and sensing, the person who did the spell could not combat as the wizard was not powerful enough and failed in order to extend the soul's surviving time for long. It was limited to five and a half days; we only have around six hours more. I can teach you the spell as it is definitely not a difficult task to perform, but we cannot waste our time." Karen spreads all the paper, cotton, woods and went to find other materials for the spell.

"Can you tell me the process first?" Stella tried to stall the spell in order to not mention Karen's daughter.

"It is all written in that spell book." Karen pointed at the thick book in front of Stella which was placed on top of a thick white pillar of the height same as Stella's hip.

Stella picked it up and flipped the pages quickly and tried to understand the steps, but she could not get it.

"It's- its- Christie." Stella said hopelessly.

"Okay then- what? Christie, but she is working for me! I mean she would ever do that!"

"Not her, hope you know what I mean." Stella placed the book back on where it belonged.

"My- daughter? It's impossible! We- cannot do it!" She yelled.

"My sister, Grace and she has been having communication through some traditional techniques, but why is it not possible?" Stella walked toward Karen.

"I am sorry Campbell but I cannot do anything. We can't save the child."
"But- why? You are here and your daughter, free her."

"It's not that easy, I cannot go against the law and we can't take any risks."
Karen looked away from Stella and walked towards the table she was setting
up for the spell to be performed.

"What do you mean by that? Ever since we were born, we have been taking
risks, didn't we?" Stella asked.

"Yeah- but let me tell you a truth, Stella Campbell. Your sister is right, everyone
are trying to save you until now. She does not even know that her life is in
more danger than that of yours since she played games with it. You should
have never returned, you were safe there in London and you were certainly
busy in a good way. This place where we wizards live and try to survive have
always tried to save our place and not play with the nature of life in an open
field where everyone are watching but you are. Your sister and you, you girls
don't know how so many wizards in the world know about you. There are
several who are hiding their identity somewhere in the corner of the world
and are even hiding. We have to manage and live a life just like humans here.
That's how we become happy, we cherish what we have and we try to live with
it. There are rules, laws, conditions and you will know it all someday. I know
that my daughter had her hand in bringing you back here and I punished her
a little but she has crossed her limits now. She did not even acknowledge the
outcome of her carelessness and I am terribly sorry about that. It's going to be
worse for both the mother and the daughter if we try to put the soul back to
the womb. I can't say much, but for you to see Dylan before you leave." Karen
bowed her head for the first time in 30 years.

"But Savannah is living with her. Who is she?" Stella asked Karen as she
doubted that Savannah might be a wizard too.

"We had to take this step. Dylan came to know about all the truth of wizards
and I believe he knows more than that. So Savannah went to look after him
by giving him medicines that will harm his past memory. When you came
back, he started remembering about Emma's death." Karen was packing all
the things and cleaning the table.

"Why are you doing all this? You cursed me 31 years ago and why are you pretending like you want to save me?" Stella stopped Karen by holding her hand and stopping her from packing up.

There was a long silence. Stella realized that she should have never asked her the question she thought because she knew Karen liked her father. Karen seemed disappointed after all she had done for Stella. She was always called wrong, bad, mean, and selfish.

"I was just doing my job as I promised to your father of saving you from your mother and it could only done by saving your sister but her death always keeps pulling her. I gave a promise to your father and no matter what, I cannot back off from it like a coward, can I?" Karen said.

"We have really less time though, can we save our sister or not?" Stella asked.

"I don't think so because she made her choice. She chose you instead of her unborn child." Karen removed Stella's hand from hers and carried the pile of books and materials on the other side of the room.

"Why is your curse so heavy on me, Karen? Why? Can you not just break it?" Stella's tears started crawling.

"I am sorry for what I have caused to you and your family. I will try to break the curse. I will try to reform the wreckage. Indeed, it will be a promise and a promise is to be fulfilled, no matter whose life goes or stays. I want you to go to Dylan now, Savannah has probably left by now and remember a thing, you don't have power but you are a magic yourself. What you think will always be right. If you want something, try to get it from your within." Karen smiled as she stepped forward towards Stella.

Stella's tears were already dry but she could not smile back at Karen.

"I am afraid to leave you alone, Stella Campbell Fontaine." Karen hugged Stella.

"Don't worry; I'll not let your promise break. I will be safe." Stella sadly after the rough night to Dylan's.

It was already 2:30 in the morning and the weather was dark and foggy. Stella was going to meet Dylan again. She had not seen him for days since the accident. To her surprise when she reached home and ringed the bell, "You know you are married right? So why are you here?" Dylan asked Stella as soon as he saw her.

Stella stared into his eyes and tried to see if who she is seeing is the person who she loved before. She got it then, the reason why she always tried to hate Dylan and never fall in love him. It was because of her, deep inside she knew it was not right to date a human. It would only cause trouble. He was arrogant, self-obsessed and mostly dauntless. He would never fear anything and would go along with his gut feeling. The reason why he knew everything about the wizard world.

"I have questions to ask you, please answer." Stella begged and Dylan let her walk in. While they were walking towards the hall where Stella first saw him reading a newspaper after eleven years, she received an unknown call. She accepted the call and asked who it was to the anonymous caller and what she got for an answer shocked her, "What?" And the phone went dead.

She closed her eyes and took a deep breath as she went back to 18 again. It was like a dream, as if she was sleeping and she could hear no one. Dylan went to the kitchen to get coffee for both of them. Stella on her own saw Emma and her again. She started hearing voices of them talking then.

"Stella, meet my cousin, Charles and Charles this is Stella. My unlucky friend. Her real name's Arlene. You can call her Arlene." Emma winked at Stella.

"Hello Arlene, ready for setting off?" Charles smiled, showing his dimples and rubbing his blond hair.

"Hi and yeah." Stella smiled back at Charles and then Emma whispered in Stella's ears," I know you will fall for him. All the girls want him, hope you don't miss it!" Stella and Emma started laughing like a little kid and it was first for Stella. The first time after three years laughing over something that actually was not true. Stella knew that she would never fall in love with Charles no matter the situation is because she could never be able to forget Dylan.

A long silence broke in, there was Dylan's voice again, "Stella! Who was on the phone?" Stella could see Dylan; she was back in her world. She realized that she was wrong about the prediction she made eleven years back. Stella knew the answer for his question that she did not know the person on the phone but her lips said something else, "It was my husband."

"Oh..okay. No further questions then." Dylan placed the cup of coffee on the table for Stella and started sipping some through his.

"He wants a divorce." Stella said without thinking. She did not like the way it sounded.

"So.. Do you want-or-like?" Dylan hesitated.

"I don't want! I mean-I don't remember him! I don't have any memory about the life I used to have when I was with him. His voice made me feel so different. I mean-I felt like I had a great past with him but I don't know. My life is just so messed up." Stella took the cup and took a sip and shook her head. She knew that she still does not remember a lot of things that happened between her and Dylan which were much more beautiful and special for both of them. She didn't remember how their love life was. Time passed so fast that she kept forgetting about Dylan once in a while because she could not love him. She did not have any right to love him and hurt him later, but that was exactly what she did. If she did not come to Dylan's life, he would have never lived a life like he was living. Staying with a wizard who made him forget about everything that was important to him. Dylan could not say anything too, because he knew that her life was messed up, but the fact that she might have had a great past with her husband, made him feel bad.

"Oh! I lost our topic. I am so sorry. How- how can we break the curse, Dylan? If you have any idea about the curse that she did on me and all because Karen said you would know." Stella said.

"I do somehow over the years after you left; I read a lot of books and journals of people who even slightly had a doubt about magicians and wizards walking around the world. I went all crazy on that once I found out about you but- I didn't know that there would be so much more to it. Families, rituals, curse, spells, laws that you call. About the curse that you have on you, it is definitely hard, but it is not impossible for you. Even your sister's unborn child that people talk about, can be saved." Dylan answered as walked around the room.

"How can I do that?" Stella raised her eyebrows and followed Dylan's movement as he walked around.

"Well.. firstly, about your sister. You know the drill, its simple magic, but there should be a very powerful wizard performing it. The curse you have one you, the answer is the cause of your curse. The person, the thing or the reason for why the curse was caused should *die* or *vanish* in your words. You are genuinely lucky that Karen is sacrificing her life for you and her almighty famous love "Edward Fontaine". Once she dies, he will come back, your family will all settle back to the way they always were around 18 years back. I still am surprised that Karen would do that because she is a highly renowned indomitable spiritual wizard." Dylan sat on the couch after being shocked himself.

"No way, that's nonsense. She is the one who cursed me not the cause of the curse." Stella claimed.

"I almost forgot to tell you. You have been slightly mistaken your whole life. The wizard who cursed on you is not Karen but Suzanne, your mother."

CHAPTER 22

Living with just a sparkle of hope

"What do you mean?" Stella was startled.

"You have a curse of catastrophe. The people who love you will always face destruction, darkness or death *like I did*." Dylan looked into Stella's eyes as she slowly sat down, realizing every bits of the suffering she had caused to many people. She sat in a deep dilemma of whom to choose. Death of a strong wizard like Karen that the wizard world needed or the destruction of the ones who loved Stella? Stella started realizing how Karen never left any evidence against her mother, Suzanne. Karen did not let Stella know the truth about the curse. Karen was guiltless, blameless and exceptionally innocent. Stella thought that she had to go back to see Karen as soon as possible.

She grabbed Dylan's wrist and pulled him, saying, "Let's hurry." They took two steps and Stella stepped turning back at Dylan who took a step back.

"It's your life, Stella. You have someone else you love and we will be strangers again. Even though I want to help you and your family, I have always wanted to, which brought me to this stage. I can't pretend not knowing a thing anymore. It's hard for me to even look at you remembering that you have someone else every other minute. I am just a friend and I don't think I am ready to accept that." Dylan looked down to his hand that Stella was holding and pulled it away.

"It's okay, I know the feeling. When you were with Madeline and every time I saw you guys together- It's all in the past now, I don't want to hurt you making you regret everything and when I heard about you and Emma, I just- I hope you do the same like I did, I did not ever let you bother about anything." Stella looked into his eyes but Dylan did not.

"You might be getting late." Dylan said softly.

Sharon smiled lightly at Dylan; there was an awkward silence between them. Stella whispered while leaving Dylan's place, "Take care, Dylan."

Dylan went back to sit on the chain and stared at Stella's half full cup of coffee. He had nothing to do anymore but only think about them, their past and his mistakes. He realized how both of them were living a different life in different countries for the past eleven years with someone else. Dylan and Savannah with an unacceptable relationship and Stella and her husband with a good relationship which was probably going to an end because of Dylan. Time just played a bad role in his life, he thought. There was no hope for Dylan anymore as he had already lost all of his second chances.

Sharon reached Karen's house again after one minute as she started getting back the magic she used to practice twelve years ago when she first got it. As she started ringing the doorbell and knocking the door, there was no sign of even a single air coming from within the house.

"Hello? Is anybody in there?" Stella asked and in a few seconds there was an answer from a familiar lady voice, "Yeah."

The door slowly was opened by Karen and Stella hugged her as soon as the door was wide open.

"Quite pleasant to see you here again, Stella. Come in" Karen left a small laugh and closed the door after both of them walked in. Stella rushed once the door was closed, checking the house thoroughly peeping into every small corner.

"Looking for something, Campbell?" Karen asked.

"Thank goodness there are no any magic materials around doing something killing thing." Stella answered breathing heavily. She finally sat down on a sofa next to the pillar that has the spell book still sitting on top.

"You are really far-sighted just like your father. We don't always need those materials to magic, we can perform rituals with our bare hands. We use our powers, not power of things." Karen laughed majestically and she stood at the opposite of Stella and smiled.

"I will never let you die because of me." Stella said seriously.

"I will take it as a very important TIL from you." She laughed again.

"What does the TIL mean?" Stella asked Karen.

"Today I learned the fact that you care a lot for me." Karen played with the curtain behind her and Stella laughed this time.

"But your death will cause havoc all over the wizard world and our families." Stella said sadly.

"Oh Campbell, I can't stand your sloppy words any longer. All I can say is that your mother is treacherous wizard." Karen smiled at Stella and stepped forward towards Stella.

"A warning?" Stella asked casually.

"It was an ultimatum." Karen whispered in Stella's left ear removing the hair blocking the ear.

Stella sighed heavily because she could not bear anymore. She could not lose another person because of her. Then Karen asked her if she had any wish that she could help with before she left. Sharon felt like there was a lump and she could not answer the question, but she has so many wishes, so many questions, demands, needed so many answers, but she asked for only one thing first, "I beg you to set my father free from the deal you guys made."

"Is that a wish or something for your sister's baby? Just a reminder, there is less than an hour left for the time." Karen warned.

"I know, but Karen, it's a wish, a request, a necessity, just once. I want to see how a mother would react. The look, her eyes, her unfaithful eyes, I want to see her whole. I want to know that I am not guilty for all the deaths have been caused for me and for anything related to me." Stella looked down and closed her fists.

"When the time comes, the clock will strike to its place." Karen said and smiled.

Stella lifted her head to look at Karen but she was left with her mouth open as she looked around the room and found herself standing in front of the mirror.

"I did not that she would just vanish like that." Stella whispered to herself. Karen Mary, Joseph would never return back to the world ever again, she thought. She would never know what would happen next. She walked back to Alex's car and as she was about to start the car, there was a knock on the windshield. Stella slowly puts down the window and saw a tall woman with dark curls, long weather jacket, high heels, a handy leather bag and a beautiful face in a woman around her 60's.

"I need to talk to you." The old lady spoke softly. Stella looked at her watch and she realized that she only had forty five minutes left.

"Madam, guess you have mistaken for who I am. I am really in a rush right now so I hope you understand." Stella smiled and turned around to get in the car again.

"I'll meet you at your home tomorrow, sharp six of your wrist watch; go to your sister fast." The lady smirked as if she knew a lot about Stella.

Stella started the car and left as soon as she got in and did not care about the lady. She reached few minutes late to home when she could hear her sister screaming her eyes out. Alex came running out of the room with Grace on his arms. Stella shook her head to Alex signing him that she could not save the child and Alex looked back at his wife sadly.

"What are you doing there? Go start the car, you drive!" Alex screamed and Stella rushed. Stella opened the main door and gave the way for Alex and rushed to open the door on the back side of the car where Grace was kept. Stella started the car as soon as Alex put Grace on his lap.

After waiting for eight years of hours, the doctor came.

"Congratulations, you've got a new princess." The doctor smiled and patted on Alex's shoulder. Alex stood there shocked with the mixture of happiness and unbelievable thing. Stella smiled at Alex and he smiled back at her with his eyes full of tears. Both of them ran to the operating room and saw the little baby they thought would be dead. Alex held Grace's hands and covered them with his. Stella smiled at them and looked at the baby girl, she was beautiful she thought. Her eyes looked so bold and looked similar like Stella's and Grace's. Stella carried the baby and played around with her. They all looked at the baby and thought if she would live or have a hard life trying to live in the human world. No one knew how she survived; she was their hope to change everything. A hope for their good future. It was like a happy ending for her sister, but it was just the beginning for Stella.

"So, this is her." A man around his 40's looked at Stella as if he was sent to kill her. Stella, the man and a lady she saw the day before was standing in front of Stella's house.

"Who is this man and who are you?" Stella asked furiously. She got frustrated as she didn't like the way the man was judging her from her appearance.

"We are here to teach you something. I mean he is but I will always be in a form in case you need any help. I can help you." The lady smiled with the wrinkles getting closer and teeth beaming.

"I'm not interested though, I have an appropriate income salary job in London. Thanks, but we don't need any job offers here, we are okay. In fact, we have a newborn baby at home that you can probably guarantee a job for after 18 years?" Stella expressed with a smirk. The lady was impressed about the way she is confident about everything but she was not there for a pity job offer but something bigger.

"Actually Karen Mary, Joseph asked us to help you train." The lady raised her eyebrows and Stella's smirk faded.

"You- you know where she is?" Stell asked curiously.

"No, she just contacted me and that's it. She didn't mention about anything, did she?" The lady answered and asked firmly. Stella shook her head.

"Maybe, yeah but who are you? I am sorry I took your appearance in a wrong way." Stella apologized.

"I am Carla Bordeaux, Karen's well-wisher and it's okay." The lady smiled.

"Good to see you Carla. So, when does this training actually start?" Stella asked.

"Today." She replied.

When Stella returned back home in the evening after the sunset, thoughts were all over her mind. She could barely lift a spoon in the air by magic, she thought it would be really hard to get to the stage where Carla blew everything in the room they were in half an hour back. As soon as she entered the hall, she could see Alex and Grace smiling and teasing the new born baby as they were cleaning her butt with tissue and changing her diaper.

"Where is Suzanne?" Stella asked them as she did not see her mother for a few days now. Alex went to the washroom to wash his hands off.

"She just went in. She was really happy to see the baby though." Grace smiled, putting the pants on to her daughter.

"Where have you been?' Alex asked as he came back again with a towel rubbing his hands.

"Um. Was just taking a long walk and met few kids. I was just telling them stories and all, you know how I am. "Stella answered, but it didn't seem like Alex or Grace cared to hear everything. They were so happy looking at their daughter. It had already been three days since the baby was born and Stella started learning magic from Carla. Stella then wondered what their family would be like when their dad returns home. Would he recognize her? What would he look like?

"What's the baby girl's name? Did you guys think about it?" Stella asked cheerfully as she sat down with the parents.

"Rebekah." Grace answered with a bright smile. Stella ooed and took the baby in her arms.

"Rebekah it is. It's perfect for a beauty like her. Rebekah Campbell Fontaine." Stella said and started playing with her for a while and handed it back to Grace to feed the baby. They had dinner together at the table without Suzanne and as soon as Stella finished washing her dishes, she went back to her room. She took a shower and went to sleep on her bed smiling. Thinking about everything that was going on, everything seemed so beautiful.

An unknown young blond guy with dimples was frowning at Stella.

"Hey, Arlene! Lift the damn bag yourself and follow me. We have to stay at the same room for a couple of days." The guy said shaking his head.

"You must be joking, I don't even know you. Let alone being in the same room as you." Stella said unacceptably.

"You will then, god damn. I am Charles Stevenson, son of one of the most well-earned CEO of the best Toy company in London. My mother passed away when I was little and since then dad never cared for me, but to send money every time I wanted to see him." There was a silence.

Stella realized that he had a hard time in life just like her. She left her home because her mother started blaming her for the family curse and all. She couldn't take it so she left home. She smiled at Charles and he looked at her, noticing the eye contact.

"What? Don't look at me that way and smile?! You aren't even in love with me or something. I said don't!" He looked pissed and annoyed.

"It's to annoy you." Stella laughed. Arlene it was. Arlene laughed. He carried her bags to the room 707 in the hotel; there weren't any other rooms so they had to stay together. That night, while Arlene slept on the bed and Charles slept on the sofa, she looked at him and glared the longest at him until she fell asleep thinking. He was beautiful, his eyes and dimples. Girls surely might have gone insane knowing he ran away with a girl like me to London. Arlene smiled by herself and closed her eyes.

"Charles.." Stella woke up finding herself on a bed as she started remembering the memories that she shouldn't have until she fix everything. She remembered when she was young hearing that if people come from another state to this state, they would forget the past if they find out about magic. Charles was the guy she ran off with eleven years ago and she fell in love with him. It was a mystery for Stella about how they married only three years ago and they were already breaking up. She started checking her phone contacts from a, b, c, d, there were a lot of names that she didn't even remember until she saw one "Mr. Hamilton". She thought she would find out everything once she calls that number. After three rings, he answered.

"Hamilton speaking, mind if you speak faster. I am busy." He said. Stella couldn't say anything, she didn't know what to say. She was dumbfounded.

"Damn- wasting my time. Hey, here to say something Veronica?-" The phone went dead after that name, Veronica.

It was 2:30 in the morning and Stella was going to Dylan's home. The weather was dark and foggy.

"You know you are married right? So, why are you here? Dylan asked as soon as he opened his door and saw her.

"I have questions to ask you. Please answer. "Stella begged.

Then there was a call for her. She accepted the call and asked who it was to the anonymous caller.

"Arlene, I thought a lot about what you said, and now, I surely know how it feels and how you might have felt. Let's get separated." Charles said.

"What?!" Stella asked in an alarming tone.

"The documents will be ready once you come back." He said and the line went dead.

That was it. Stella has asked him for divorce before she came back to Texas.

The night slowly fell in pieces, she understood everything. She was still cuddling in her bed, eyes gloomy.

> *"It's like the first word your sister slammer.*
> *The first touch of a cub, like seeing a mother giving birth to a baby.*
> *Like tuning into the song that is similar to your story.*
> *And in a second of this wonderful world.*
> *There is a switch and you forget all of it*
> *You just fall and fall so deep,*
> *When someone asks you how you felt?*

You can't even explain because there is nothing that you remember
of the world being beautiful.
Nothing so precious like you were the only person on Earth.
All left is you and your body with no soul.
The smile is taken away from you.
There is no love, care, hope or rejoicement left in the dead soul."

The next day Stella hurried to the place she met Carla and as soon as she reached the house, Carla entered the hall, "Early today, Campbell? Any problem?"

"Yeah, I mean.. Carla.. the boundary of magic people talk about. The memory that people lose when entering and knowing about the magic world, I am regaining those memories that I shouldn't. What does that mean?" Stella asked and Carla's face went into shock and realization. She started panicking right after.

"I forgot to retrain the boundary of power with the other wizards. I am supposed to supervise, how could I forget such an important thing? It's going to take more than just a day to get everyone together and inform them. The wizards don't even leave a single trace to track their location. How am I going to face the superiors. It does not mean anything, it just means that I made a mistake." Carla sighed.

"Sure, but-" Stella was saying when Carla vanished. She did not want to forget any of what she remembered. She wanted to know more. She then realized that if she rested her mind, then maybe again, she could remember everything in just one day. Before Carla would stop the memory erasing power, Stella could remember a lot by then.

She closed her eyes and took a deep breathe.

"Arlene, you will be working in this office, you are the assistant of that guy there. You are basically just a normal staff like anyone else but you will get promoted soon so don't bug me. A car will be waiting for you outside at 9 tonight. There are maids in our house so there shouldn't be any problem with cleaning and hygiene.

"Are we living together, again?" Arlene asked with wide eyes.

"We are just- living together. Nothing else." He said.

"Okay, I won't disappoint with my work." Arlene said and went to her table. She was working very hard. That was her life.

Stella opened her eyes as she figured that she could not put too much stress and try to remember all of her past. Her head was aching. Then Stella thought of doing something, taking a big step. She made her mind to be the Arlene, she was for the past eleven years. She booked a place for London once she reached home and started packing her bags.

Without telling anyone she flew back to London. She flew back to her unknown life she wanted to know desperately. She went back to Charles and left Dylan and his memories behind. The time would be still for the time being until she comes back because Carla said that is what would happen. Carla would call her back when the days would be back to same time again.

Stella left her hometown, again.

CHAPTER 23

Recollection of the past

Stella stepped off the jet and there was a tall, lovely woman looking at her and heading towards her.

"Arlene! How are you, darling?" The face seemed familiar and cheerful to Stella but she couldn't recognize the person. She had never seen her before.

Then there was a blurring of vision. A loud noise and Stella closed her eyes. Stella opened her eyes and her eye color turned to a lighter color than her natural once. She looked around and then she saw her, Sally. Charles's elder sister who she was really close to.

"I am fine, how are you and how did you find out that I am coming?" Arlene asked.

"Oh, Arlene. My agency called." Sally laughed and they went home together.

Sally and Arlene were neighbors and good friends as well apart from being relatives. Arlene used to look after Sally's daughter Janet sometimes as a baby sitter. Sally's husband was Calvin Muller was also very close to Arlene. Sally was adorable, friendly, cheerful, happy and a very smart woman. As they were in the car going home, Sally told everything that had happened while Arlene was absent. Sally hires a stupid maid who did nothing but sit every ten minutes, about Janet not getting good scores for her last test, about the expenses going higher and higher for everything.

While Arlene was taking out the key and trying to unlock the door, she suddenly stopped.

"Wait a second." Arlene whispered and dropped her bag. She rubbed her forehead back and forth a couple of times.

"Charles called me when I was away and he asked for a divorce. He didn't even care to hear me out. We are getting separated Sally! I can't believe that." Arlene said.

"It's okay. It's what you wanted for a long time. I thought you would be happy." Sally replied sadly because she was scared that there wouldn't be much reason for her to visit Arlene again. If she did, her brother would hurt.

"Sorry Sally, I think I'll take it from here. Thank you for coming." Arlene smiled.

"Any time, darling. Take care of yourself." Sally turned around and left.

Arlene looked back at the door and turned around the key to open it. She had to go in. She thought of spending some time with Charles. She went in with all her bags and luggage after entering the password of the second door. The password was 1710. Their anniversary date.

They were as excited and happy as every other couple would be on their wedding day, Arlene remembered her beautiful wedding dress was gorgeous. She planned to make some of Charles's favorite dishes as she went to the kitchen after taking a shower. She couldn't even remember the last time they had lunch or dinner together. She started getting nervous about how to react when he comes back home. She prepared the food taking two hours and started practicing the words she would say to him out loud until they sounded convincing.

"Arlene? Hey." Arlene heard Charles voice as she woke up. She was lying down on the couch.

"Hey, I was actually waiting for you. I made dinner." Arlene said as she stood up rearranging the pillows on the sofa.

"Yeah, I saw it. It smells good, I'll arrange them." Charles went to the kitchen. Arlene cursed herself for not waiting for her husband, but falling asleep. She was tired after the long flight. Charles brought everything and served the food by himself to both of them. They silently started eating.

"What's the occasion?" Charles broke the silence.

"We are getting separated." that was the occasion, Arlene slightly smiled.

"When are you getting back to work?" Charles asked.

"Probably tomorrow." She knew that he would ask her about work because they were complete workaholics. They would always talk about finances, work, power and meetings every time they talked for the last few months.

Arlene started taking wine, pouring it, drinking it, finishing it, pouring again, drinking again and finishing another glass again. Charles noticed her eyes getting red. He didn't know what was going on in her mind that she was simultaneously taking wine and finishing it. Then finally Arlene smiled after taking seven cups.

Charles looked at her and thought she was still very beautiful like the first time he saw her. She was always one of those girls who would look twice at a handsome guy passing by her when she was 18 and he had just seen her for the first time. He never wanted to fall in love with her, but there wasn't any guarantee of not to. He fell in love with her every time he saw her and he was still falling in love with her, he knew that he could never be able to stop it. She would get anyone after their divorce, indeed she had a lover in Texas who was waiting for her, he thought. She would get the most successful man in all over the places she goes to. There would be someone who would give her everything and support her for everything she wanted. Arlene would fade away from his world soon.

Arlene was still smiling at Charles and it seemed less like a married lady, but a young woman who was single. Three years of a marital life and divorce, that was a very common thing to happen in every relationship. There were hundreds of men and women walking, working, earning hard even after their hardship of divorce and both Charles and Arlene would get over that easily like them.

Then Arlene spoke, "Charles, do you remember a book name 'The lost person'? Perhaps, not. The first time I read that book was in a public library, it had one of the most eye-catching and interesting front cover I have ever seen in any of the books It was lying there for over 20 years on the bookshelf Row No. 11, rack three. When I was registering my name to borrow it, you know what happened? Your name was on it. You were the last person who had borrowed that book and I really did not want to fill mine it too. It was surprising and unexpected, but you were always unexpected for me, don't you think so? That time, I did not love you but- I don't know.. I wanted my name to get registered just below yours, so I did. I filled my name and every time I read that book. It reminded me of you, that distinguishable handwriting of yours which I loved to read when we were in love and you used to leave a letter behind the flower pot of my bedroom every weekend. It's funny." Arlene took another sip of wine in sorrow and her eyes were full of tears.

Charles did not stop her because he did not want to. He wanted to know what she felt for him and what was buzzing her.

"I then finally went back to the librarian one day, not to return the book, but to make it mine forever. I wanted to keep it. I wanted to read the novel again and again, over and over forever. Strange right? I promised that I would return it when I am over us and I am ready to forget you." Arlene went to sleep. Charles held her hands as she was moving hastily, placed her on the bed and sat next to her.

Arlene kept mumbling while she was sleeping and Charles watched his wife falling asleep. He could only stare at her pretty face. He agreed with himself that he would leave her as there was no option. She loved someone else and he forced her to love him. They were always more devoted and concerned about their work than getting jealous of one another flirting with another person. There weren't any feelings left. Charles covered her body with the quilt and he fell asleep right beside her.

The next day, Charles woke up at five in the morning and saw his wife still sleeping. He did not need any alarm clock especially after he had faced an entire week of challenges in office. He took a shower and Arlene woke right then. Arlene took a shower in her room while Charles started preparing breakfast for both of them. He left the house when Arlene was changing her clothes.

When Arlene entered the office after parking her car in the lot, as she walked on her way to her chair the staffs greeted her and she finally felt happy.

"Welcome back, Ms. Stevenson." Her assistant greeted as soon as she entered her cabin.

"Good Morning Greta, long time." Arlene smiled.

"Long time indeed after six years because you never took any leaves." Greta smiled brightly. Greta was a great friend of Arlene after Carla.

After the hectic day covering all the appointments Arlene has missed, she dropped Greta at her place and Arlene planned on getting some fresh air hanging out. On the way she crossed lots of homeless, poor, runaways and she remembered her past.

She would have never fallen in love with Charles if it weren't for these people, a day when they were together in her car after his car met an accident. He suggested her to go for a walk with him to somewhere she hadn't ever been. It was a one hour walk and she would have never walked that long in her life but that certain she did. She walked with Charles. The person she had chosen to spend her years with. They walked to the street of homeless and poor and Arlene couldn't believe how much Charles loved helping them.

After six years of staying with Charles she was close to know him that particular day when she was 24. She saw Charles donating money to the poor. All the street people knew his great name, Mr. Stevenson, she found out that he used to donate money to the organization every week without failing and it had already been three years. She couldn't believe her eyes at first seeing at this rich Stevenson she was living with for all these years without knowing how soft his heart was.

Later, while they were on their way to their home, she came to know that every month he used to donate 50,000 to the charity, every week he used to do a 5-10 hours social working on Fridays working at the home center for the poor, working for them, serving food as a social worker. She had never seen this part of him. She thought to herself how good- hearted, simple, humble, sincere, hard-working, innocent and beautiful he was from inside. It would have taken her life to know someone like him. She thanked god and Emma to send her to a hand of a man like Charles.

Since, that day she always started going to the home center every Friday. She noticed Charles wouldn't miss a day. She didn't have many friends except for the people from the office. Then she had come to know lots of people, social workers working in the home center. A lot of people helped her in explaining her work they have been doing for several years.

Then she remembered Veronica Grogan, who had started working there from her childhood, probably since 15 years old. She worked for her father, her father were a social worker himself, who involved his daughter in the world of poor, introducing the life she had never seen. Veronica was very soft hearted being with the poor for ten years. She knew the names of two halves of the people coming to get food and a room to share with ten. All the social workers were good to her; she was a great person in her early age. Veronica was beautiful herself with those blonde hair working for 8000 people in the home center. All the poor, homeless had their own stories of getting into the street life. They were robbed, bankrupt, cheated, raped, tortured, thrown away, and murdered. Murdered in a sense, some people trying to kill the person and they escaped somehow and their family had never seen them since then, they were registered 'dead'. They weren't counted among the other people; they had no official sir name, citizenship, money, clothes, land. They used to sleep on the street side, under the bridge, the door of the malls, shops and houses.

Arlene knew a lot of poor, homeless people. The homeless used to move from one place to another, they didn't like to be at a particular spot for long as they feared to be recognized by someone. Arlene would always thank god for she was not one of them and for knowing that these people even existed. Arlene finally reached their home, Stevenson's home. It was Monday and she thought to herself if the last Friday Charles might have gone to the home center by himself all alone as for a few months earlier they used to go together. As she entered the house, she could see Charles relaxing at the sofa with a glass of wine, of course. She then realized that she hadn't seen Charles at the office like most often as their office were situated at different ends of the office, they could hardly see one another at the office working, Charles glanced at her when she came in closing the door. Arlene then started talking as most of the time she had to start their topic; Charles never started any conversation between them.

"Hey, how was work today?" Arlene smiled and took off her heels.

"Fine, how was yours?" Charles didn't make any eye contact.

"Hectic schedule, must say, one after other appointments. Lot of new plans on the new project. The terms were changed, was it?" Arlene asked.

"Yeah, it was."

"On my absence, I assure that the partners are planning great and horrible. They don't take our suggestions anymore." Arlene looked pissed.

"The terms- we suggested it."

"Oh really? But- just think of the future, the project has to be a great one. It has taken two years and at the end- why change? I mean- it isn't thinking of the future ahead. Everything will be shut. Our invested money, the government's tax all will be gone in thin air." Arlene suggested.

"We will talk about it tomorrow. The other staffs are probably discussing about it and how to turn it into a great one." Charles didn't seem interested at all and that bothered Arlene.

"Hope so." She wasn't sure if he would mention about it ever. He liked hiding things better.

Then Arlene thought for a while that they had tried for a baby, but she always used to take pills, pills to stop the baby and Charles didn't know about that. She checked her handbag if there were any more pills left, but there weren't any. It had been more than a month she had stopped taking pills and it just scared her. She wasn't ready for a baby.

"Mrs. Stevenson sorry to disturb you, but- I got a call that Mr. Stevenson wants to see you in his cabin." Greta walked in after knocking the door.

"Personally?" Arlene looked puzzled. "I think so… why would he have called you then?" Greta said amazingly.

Arlene smiled, "I'll be there in fifteen minutes." Greta left the office and Arlene thought for a while and went to Charles office. She had her count and she realized the last time she entered his office was nearly seven months back but it was still the same, just the files on the rack has changed, "You asked for me?" Arlene asked softly looking at her busy husband, boss in the office.

Arlene entered in with a slight voice. Charles looked kind of busy to Arlene. He looked at her once and then closed the file he was going through. Then he glanced at her as if seeing his wife for the first time in years, "Actually, yeah, you were having some problem with the Project, weren't you?"

"Yeah" Arlene looked quite shocked.

"I just wanted to say that I don't have much time for that little project. You have to go to talk to the trustee about it, if you aren't yet satisfied." He said briefly.

"But the trustee is-"

"Gone somewhere else for a couple of weeks. I know things going around better than you do, Mrs. Stevenson." His voice harsh like he didn't know she is his wife.

"Then how can we make decisions? I mean- the project plan has to be changed! The building will collapse with thousands of people working in there!"

"That's your problem."

"Repeat the words again Charles." Arlene walked forward.

"It's your problem, the project. Do you have any more questions, doubts, dissatisfaction?" Charles raised his voice.

"You're horrible! You aren't this. You at least weren't this! You are hopeless." Arlene went back to her office all frustrated.

Charles had changed a lot. She could never forget him, she had lots of other work to focus on but she couldn't stop thinking about the project that was building a large society of home for the poor people, more than half of the work was complete and only the decorations and furniture works were left. She had a very big hand on it and she didn't want to cause any trouble. Then she called her secretary.

"Yes, ma'am. I guess you want to talk and discuss about the Project but sorry to say Mrs. Stevenson, the building is almost done and the project is closed." Greta spoke fast in her strong accent. Something she always liked about her secretary.

"Great, how can they finish the work in two months? How could they? I didn't look at it for few months and they have blown everything already?" Arlene looked unsatisfied.

"There are 250 laborers on the project if they work hard enough its possible. You need not worry, you should keep on checking the news, the project will be a great success. Actually, the upper heads in a short notice told us to finish the work that has been pending for two years." Greta informed.

"I'll see, but I don't have a good feeling about it. There's something wrong." Arlene suspected.

The next day,

Arlene madly went to Charles cabin. She had just checked the news and there was something more than incredible. For a moment she wanted to kill her husband. She thought to herself, he would be the reason for everything, everything that had happened. She could not control herself for the first time in her whole life. She was mad. She pushed the door hard and entered the cabin without asking or knocking. Second time in seven months and she was a thunder, "See what you have done?!"

"What now?" Charles looked tired.

"That building! 30 are injured!" Arlene cried.

"Why are you telling me this? The company will give the insurance to the families." He sounded careless.

"It's 30 of them, Charles, and they are all in a bad condition, more 20 of them are sick and in a tremendous stage. You still don't care?" Arlene raised her eyebrows. She was more than shocked by his sentence. She needed an answer, an answer for his annoyance.

"Yes, I do, of course. They were working for our company and we are at a loss and the answer probably is I care."

"All you care about is money. You have no humanity left in you. You were so different back then."

"You may leave now. I have lots of other projects to deal with." He went through his pile of files.

"Even I am not that free to talk about the project but what happened? All the people who are suffering all the families who have lost their hope of getting a happy life, it's all because of you. You are someone who approves all the projects in the office. You killed their hope, all of them. Something made you go so cold blind." Arlene rolled her eyes and shook her head.

Arlene went back to her cabin all startled. Her life was all complicated then, but nothing went the way she thought it would go like. Arlene couldn't concentrate on her work. She took a leave and went to see all the injured victims in the hospital. She could not control her tears. The family members were moaning all over the floor. They had no one to feel their pain and to look after them anymore. All the members of the victim could be homeless within a week if they aren't healthy and strong.

CHAPTER 24

Without any utterance

Arlene's P.O.V:

I just can't believe this. How can a man be this heartless all of a sudden?

"Stella." there was a whisper from behind. It sounded like a voice I have heard of before. I turned around slowly to see who's there.

I see myself standing at the opposite side of the wall. It's a new world. I see a lot of people around me passing by in a rush. I am not in a hospital but at school? A high school? I see a young me, but she seems so sad? And she is crying? But why? I want to know why I'm crying, if it's me. She looks so pretty. I never thought I was that pretty when I was young. She is reading a letter and her eyes are bloodshed. I lean into her back to read it, read the letter. The letter seems to be old and all crumbled.

Stella,

> *I'm sorry for what I've done to you so far. The way I've always treated you all this time. I never knew that Dylan liked you. He never told me. All I knew was that he liked a girl and she liked him too but I wanted him all by myself. This is one of the reasons I never wanted to know who that other girl was. The girl Dylan*

liked a lot. The girl he used to text 24/7. Even though I didn't know who she was, I've always been jealous of her existence. It made me feel like I was really far from Dylan even though he was right next to me. He never smiled at my texts but he always did when he gets her messages. It's been a month since I found out that the girl was you, Stella. You never told me about this. I wanted to shout at you and get mad at you for making Dylan fall head over heels for you but it's not only your fault, it's his too. I didn't know you much but because of Dylan I got close to you and that's when I found out that you liked him too. I always knew that there's something about you that bugs me. I didn't know that it would be this. I'm sorry for I want Dylan all by myself but I think you like him too much for you wanted him to be happy all these time. Dating Dylan was not something I could've dreamt of but he was all I wanted. Thank you for you stood back, stepped a step backward and let me go along with him. I heard you gave up on him after a year which was why he started asking me out. When you read this, I probably won't be there with you. So, please forgive me for telling you to leave. I'm really thankful towards your effort. I would never be able to be this strong to let go of someone I love so much. I have cancer and all I want is Dylan by my side, I want to forget your existence during my last breath. So, please understand my emotions. Take care and stay safe.

Emma Block.

Who is Emma? Who is Stella? Who is Dylan? Who are all these people? And why is she crying reading this letter? They were my friends? Do I know them? I've never heard of these names before. Where am I? What is this place? It's not London for sure. Then what is this place? Could it be somewhere near London? Possibly.

She slowly walks past the building of the school down the road takes a bus and enters a house. It's a small world indeed. There are her family members. She has a sister. Do I have one? I never knew that. If this is my past, then maybe I do have a sister. No dad at home, no mom. I see her mom coming. Looks like her, actually me.

"What're you doing here by yourself? Let's go home honey. What's gone can't be changed." She smiles warmly.

Stella quickly hides the letter by crumbling it into her left palm. She wipes her tears and goes to her room with her mother.

Where am I?

A guy comes from behind with my sister; I can see his back as he's facing towards them. He is tall, blue jeans, brown boots, leather jacket and very thick voice.

"Can I talk to Stella?" I hear him say and the older lady which is my mom nods looking at the young Stella.

The two of them sit on the sofa, lying next to the bed and stay quiet for five minutes. The mother and sister leave the room and go downstairs.

"I am really sorry about Emma's death. She was one of your closest friends." Dylan looks at her.

"She still is." The girl who looks like me replies and behind her hand, she is still holding on to that sheet of paper the dead girl left by. The only thing that I found out by this scene is that I was the reason for... her death.

The vision got clear and someone pushed me away.

"Doctor! Doctor! Look at my son, what has happened to him? He just collapsed while we were talking. He has a very weak heart, please do something! Tell me he's going to be alright. "A mother cried, begging for her son's life.

I'm in the hospital where tons of people are dying tonight and among all the deaths in the world, I was the reason for one of them. I ran away from my town because I killed someone. I killed my best friend when I was 18. I killed her and I am scared that it's not the only thing; I might have caused something bigger than what I'm seeing.

I slowly get back all the memories of my hidden life.

Evan, Chloe, Grace, Emma, Dylan, Dave, Isaac, Charles, Jacob, Elijah, my family.

Things don't always work the way you want them to. That's what I have been told throughout my life. We shouldn't expect more than what we can have, that's what I've been warned about. I have always listened to those people and acted according to their suggestions but this time? I think I want more. I want Dylan to be beside me holding my hands and telling me that, "It'll be fine. You can do it. We can do it together now and forever."

Should I hope for this to happen? Is it too much for a wish? Is it too much to come true?

All I can do is expect as less as I can but this is the least I can ask for at the moment. I want him to be here, next to me, his presence would be enough for days. Enough to forget all the deaths I have caused throughout my life. His hug would comfort me enough for me to make myself believe that he will protect me from myself, from my misfortune, from my bad luck, from the all the evil spirit. And you know what they say, 'When we are hurt, It's our past. We can either run from it or hide from it...'

I just can't agree to hide from it. It's what made me, made me who I am now. Everyone in this wizard world knows about me for my past and for my future as well.

Will there ever be someone who would be there for me throughout all these hardships. I don't want any heartache anymore. I want to live.

I wake up to the dog barks around and birds chirping above me. The morning air chilled me to the bone, forcing me to pull the sleeves of my sweater covering my warm fist. I breathe, enjoying the fresh and windy air that was like tranquility to my lungs. Rubbing my eyes firmly, I took a second look at the little naughty girl climbing down the Neon colored slide, I had been ignoring for a while when I doze off. I liked babysitting Janet, as in Charles niece whom I consider my niece as well; she was more like a sister to me. I leaned back to the chair I have been sitting on for about an hour. I am used to it, this hard cold old fashioned wooden bench as I come here every Saturday for my part-time. Yeah, as weird as it sounds I get paid for babysitting my aunt's daughter. I have never worked for free, never would.

Slowly, I turned towards my right. It was one of the old man living in the neighborhood next to the noisy park. I kept looking in his direction, as if I knew what would come next. Entering the park with his exhausted, worn-out face that somehow still managed to smile. I took a deep breath and stood up. With my Louis Vuitton bag on my right shoulder, I approached the old man and coughed. This old man always has the best story to share and I could only raise my eyebrows to state my disbelief. I made sure that my face did not show any sign of shock or surprise. I always nodded unnaturally to everyone despite how devastated their unusual story might have sounded like.

"Classic, Stella." Someone's voice called.

I turned around quickly, trembling, a fear rose within myself wondering if someone in this country knew about the real me.

I could see no one behind me except for some kids arguing for the see-saw seat. A lot of things were going on since last few weeks; I had to go back to my country for my family.

About the project that caused havoc and killed several people, it actually turned out as a dream for me to remember my past. No one died, nothing happened. It was all just a dream and I didn't know what to say about it. It was such a bad dream. It was terrible.

Nevertheless, I still want to go back now. I can go just by my magic now. It's still not too late to forgive and forget everything. I signed the divorce paper and sent it to Charles already. I am sure Charles will marry Veronica sooner or later. They look great together, I have always noticed it.

"I am leaving London tomorrow, Greta." I smiled at Greta and she looked surprised as well as sad.

"You just returned." Greta replied sadly.

"I won't ever come back here." I patted on her right arm and started packing my files.

"My mom won't let me get another job because she thinks that I am not capable of painting." She said.

"Hey, I have seen your paintings. They are amazing and am sure that if you start a business by yourself, then you will be a very successful woman. About your mom? Parents don't always know everything about you. They act like adults, but we never know what they are scared of. It might be something minor like a bug, too. It's a strange world. You need to show them what you are capable of." I smiled at her and carry the box of files. I walked away from my cabin as Greta followed me.

"I will definitely try." She smiled, waving towards me.

I looked back at my cabin for one last time and headed towards Charles office, but he wasn't there. His assistant said that he took a leave for today and she can't contact him anymore. It wasn't unexpected, but I wanted to see him for the last time, so I went back home with my office things.

I walked inside and saw Sally sitting on the couch with Janet. There were four cups of coffee and one black tea on the table. I smiled at Sally and Janet and walked straight to my room without saying a word.

As I entered my room, I saw Charles and Veronica standing there in front of the window talking to each other. It was too soft that I couldn't hear but I didn't dare to break into them and get mad at him because I wouldn't want to ruin our time. It was our time to say goodbye.

"Hey" I walked in with a smile as if it was all fine and good. Both of them turned around to look at me and Veronica got anxious the second she saw me.

"Hi, Arlene." She managed to speak after taking a gulp. She doesn't realize how powerful I am since I am a wizard. My power of sensing is much higher than the average level and I am definitely not pleased with that blessing we have got.

"I just wanted to talk to Charles for a bit, if you don't mind." I grinned and Veronica nod.

"You don't have to feel uncomfortable or awkward. It's okay to be with him." I assured her while she was leaving just to make her feel less insecure.

"So that's it." Charles looked at me, still standing where he was a few minutes ago.

"Yeah, I am planning to go back to my country and be with my family." I told him.

"Have a good life, Arlene. No matter where you are or who are with, I hope you are always happy." Charles walked forward and we hug each other.

"I think we underestimated the power of love we share." I joked behind his ears and we both laugh together.

"Yeah, I guess you are right." He said while pulling away the hug.

We start walking out of the room as he helps me to pull my luggage. I hadn't even unpacked half of my stuff and I am already leaving him. I hug everyone and while I was leaving, Sally and Janet started crying like a little baby. Charles dropped me to the airport and I didn't really have to take the plane.

I vanish like other wizards into the thin air because I am one.

As soon as I reached my home, I check the date. The time was forwarded to the day I last left this town. I had to try to break the curse.

If I had to give up my life for that, I would never hesitate to take that step.

As I was chanting the prayers I learned from the great wizards and using the spell book of Karen in front of our yard, I see a man walking.

He somehow looked familiar to me from far.

"Hi, I hope you didn't forget me again this time." Dylan smiled like always, he was back to normal. Since, the wizard girl who was looking after him had to leave and he had this life changing event where he remembered everything and told me several magic languages that I didn't even know. He is finally back.

"Hi, I'm Stella and I am sorry, but who are you?" I smiled back at Dylan. His eyes widened in surprise, I could read his mind. The time stood still and I kept staring at him, how could I have been so unaware of his love for such a long time. How could I give up on him and live a better life of my own? He was waiting for me for the past ten years.

As the time started to tick again, I could feel him starting to stumble. He took few steps towards me, pushing away some twigs that were stopping him from taking any step further.

He exhaled, "I wanted you to know that, I.. um.. Ste.. Stella, for once I want you to listen to my voice. I know that you are somewhere deep inside and I want you to know that I have liked you from the very beginning. In the corridors, I saw you doing magic once, but I pretended like I never saw it. I was scared I would lose you. Even though, I never wanted to hurt you and since the day we started talking I made sure I didn't show any of my flaws to you. No matter how many times I tried to hide it, you always found them and you started believing in false words. You told me that you would never want to like me, that you would always hate me but it never worked that way. You never could do anything that you promised you would because deep inside you know, you are wrong and you want the evidence to prove it. You wouldn't listen to anyone and never cared about how people point their fingers towards me at times. You flatly looked into my eyes and never failed to surprise me on how much you could trust me. You were a nice, beautiful and a bold girl, but what I now see is a very different person. I never wished to change you but emotionally, I always did. I am not sure that by telling all these, I'll ever see you again or not, but every time you forgot the memories of us, it was really hard for me. I never stopped looking for you in the crowd and I would never be able to because you are different, you appeared all of a sudden in front of me and changed my world and you just vanish. I want you to stay, I always did."

Surprisingly, I took a step towards him too, because the words he said, were the ones I have always wanted to hear. Leaving no space amongst one another, except for our breaths, I asked "Why did you never tell me that you knew about the real me?"

"I was afraid that you would make me forget about you." Our eyes met each other.

"Oh." I smiled, realizing that he did the right thing.

"You.. you can't do any of those, right? I was always curious about that." He laughed out this time, feeling more comfortable with the uneven atmosphere.

"I can." I giggled.

"You won't make me forget anything right?" He asked.

"I will have to think about that." I smiled, turning back and arranging the leaves.

"Can.. I hug you before anything happens?" He asked.

"Yeah, sure." I replied.

As the time started to tick again between us, I could feel his warmth right next to me, trying to speak up for me. He didn't want to explain everything about us again to me, I always tried to forget him and it always worked. He was tired of trying to lead me to a good life with him. All these explanation about us would take a decade, more even and he was tired of explaining every single memory of us time and again.

"What if I tell you that I remember you?" I teased him.

"I would ask you to marry me." Dylan answered with a smirk.

"What if I say no?" I asked again smiling.

"That would never happen." He bragged as if there wouldn't be any chance. Well, yeah, there wouldn't, but we could fight against it together if something happens.

"Are you sure, Mr. Dylan Edward Darrington?" I asked in a weird accent that I wasn't sure about myself.

"Perhaps, Ms. Stella Campbell Darrington." He giggled. It was a proposal I hope. We both laughed as we try to forget our horrible past. We look back at the book and try to end the curse fully.

I felt like I was finally living.

"How is your dad?" He asked while I sat down tired.

"I don't know." I whispered.

"Do you know where he is?" He sat beside me.

"I don't know. I don't know anything about him but that he is safe and he should be able to come back to us. But he won't. After all these years, I don't think that he is courageous enough to come back to the family he left behind decades before. I don't even know what he looks like right now. My father. What must it feel like to have a father who loves me? I don't even remember the last time we smiled or spoke. What about you?" I turned to look at him as we were breathing the fresh air and the noise of the city that had grown so much.

"My dad. I never had one. My mom was my everything until she was declared brain dead when she was having a surgery. I was in university. Can you imagine, getting a surgery and hoping for a healthy person or the deseased person back but hearing that she was brain dead on the table with her flesh wide open? I always asked myself, how could she even die? How could she leave me alone with no one? Then I got the answer from her diary. It said that she was the one who broke up with my dad and she kept me a secret when she was pregnant. She did not love any man. She only wanted a heir to be just like her and have all of her property." He ended softly with a shake of head as his tears dropped. The question about my father's wherabouts still lingered in my ears.

"I'm sorry for pouring out such petty issues about my life when you lived your life without knowing your father even existed, falling in love with a girl who always tried to flip back at you, being a prisoner in your own house for eleven years and living your life through hell." I apologized and wiped his tears off.

"Your father was a jerk and so was my mom. My father never tried to find me and your mother never accepted you. So, that makes the two of us." He smiled as he looked away.

"Hey, we are okay. We both are okay. Both of our parents were bad and that does not mean everyone are like them. We will be different. Everyone is different. I shouldn't have told you these silly things about myself. It's nothing compared to yours." I held his hands and assured him.

"It's okay. You should always tell me. I am the one who is capable enough to be the candidate to hear you out because I will be a constant reminder of how miserable life can be and that you will overcome it. We will overcome it together." He looked at me with those beautiful eyes.

We should not always think of the worst case scenario to make ourselves feel better, it struck my mind. It's already hard to get what we want without earning it. We could try to be happy. For the first time, I remembered everything and he didn't try. He was a human and I could do nothing to change the fact. It's okay to love someone whatever they are born as, no one gets to choose. But we get to choose who we will spend the rest of our lives with and I don't want to make the same mistake that my mother did. So, when we get the chance to whether be with them or not, no one should hesitate or worry if the society will judge you. Life is filled with struggles and miseries, but we need to learn to live with it by fighting for the people we care for. The curse my mom put on me is far gone and no one will get harmed because of me, I will never be the reason for any mishaps or destructions. I will be happy.

Dylan looked at me in the eye and smiled.

I think it is important for everyone to know that they are not the only one who are hurting for small things, everyone does at some point and it is okay to be hurt and to feel that way. Dylan was hurting. I was too, I still am, but hurting lasts a lifetime, happiness do not. I want to embrace the happiness for this one time and try to make it last for as long as I can imagine.

I wanted Dylan to know that I wanted our kids to be human, not a cursed wizard and we could definitely make that possible if we formed a team of two because he is a genius and I'm not. I'm just, me.

I put my head on top of his shoulder and we smiled with the thin air for the change we will bring to our lives. We will. We have to.

It all seemed too surreal.

'Happy New Year: New Year, New me.'

Printed in the United States
By Bookmasters